THE SUNDAY OF LIFE

THE SUNDAY OF LIFE

a novel by

RAYMOND QUENEAU

Translated from the French by

BARBARA WRIGHT

A NEW DIRECTIONS BOOK

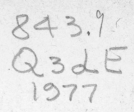
© Librairie Gallimard, 1952
Copyright © 1977 by Barbara Wright

Manufactured in the United States of America
Originally published in French as *Le Dimanche de la vie* by Librairie Gallimard in 1952
First published clothbound and as New Directions Paperbook 433 in 1977

Library of Congress Cataloging in Publication Data

Queneau, Raymond, 1903–76
    The Sunday of life.
    (A New Directions Book)
    Translation of Le Dimanche de la vie.
    I. Title.
PZ3.Q325su4   [PQ2633.U43]   843'.9'12   76–49628
ISBN 0–8112–0645–9
ISBN 0–8112–0646–7 pbk.

New Directions Books are published for James Laughlin
by New Directions Publishing Corporation,
333 Sixth Avenue, New York 10014

INTRODUCTION
"Polocilacru"

I USED to think it was a sad fate for a modern writer to have reached the pinnacle of fame, or whatever, when people all over the place were already writing theses about him. But I think I'm changing my mind. So far at least eight theses have been written about Raymond Queneau in America, three in England, seven in France, one in Rumania, one in Italy, and others elsewhere. It's since I've observed what the casual critics of even the so-called "quality" papers write about him, and compared it with the opinions and knowledge of people who have studied him, that I have begun to think that the more people who study him the better. Provided, of course, that they don't make their studies too serious, too pedantic, too plodding, and above all, too humorless—and you can never tell, with thesis writers.

Queneau is still, to some extent, considered the "enfant terrible" of French literature, though he is not exactly an "enfant" any more—he was born in 1903. But he is also a philosopher, a mathematician, a historian, an encyclopedist, even a painter—and he puts all of himself into all of his novels. Above all, he is a poet—he has always maintained that he sees no essential difference between prose and poetry. Encompassing and penetrating his gifts, talents, traits, interests, however, is his humor. And that is why academic analysis of him sometimes cuts its own throat, because humor, treated in that way, tends to sneak away and laugh up its sleeve.

The Sunday of Life (*"Le Dimanche de la vie"*), Queneau's tenth novel, was published in 1951, and everyone is agreed in calling it one of his "happiest" and "sunniest" books. Also, one of his most enjoyable. But what actually is an "enjoyable" novel? Surely not just one that we read to pass the time. And even less, one which relieves us of the obligation of having to think. Queneau himself has a much higher opinion of the reader than that: far from considering him a half-witted, passive consumer, he takes the view that he is an active partner in the Happening that is a book. More than thirty years ago he wrote: "After all, why shouldn't we demand a certain effort from the reader? We always explain everything to him. In the end, he gets fed up with seeing himself so contemptuously treated."

The "effort" Queneau expects the reader to want to make, and which is so closely allied to the "enjoyment" of reading him, is basically, I think, an effort of the imagination. And the more we read and re-read him, the more easily this effort of the imagination comes to us, in exactly the same way as we learn how to understand our good friends, with all their quirks, qualities, foibles, and idiosyncrasies, merely through prolonged acquaintance with them. With Queneau, of course, the French have the advantage over us, because they can get to know all sides of him by reading his poems, short stories, essays—on history, mathematics, linguistics, and other subjects —whereas only a limited number of his novels (and nothing else) has so far been translated into English. Even so, enough is available, I think, for the interested reader to get a good idea of Queneau's quality and scope. And I feel—and the French *know*—that he is one of the most interesting, important, and original writers of today.

Though *The Sunday of Life* is set in one of the most traumatic of recent periods—1936–40, the dark years leading up to the Second World War and including its outbreak in Europe up to the fall of France; and though the book makes frequent references to the history of that time—the Popular Front in France with its welfare laws, for instance; it nevertheless does indeed manage to be one of Queneau's happiest, sunniest and most undated novels: it far transcends anything like a mere chronicle of the times.

Queneau's epigraphs are never accidental, and the quotation from Hegel that introduces *The Sunday of Life* gives essential clues to the understanding of the book. It comes from *The Philosophy of Fine Art*, Volume III, Subsection III,

Chapter I, and then quite a few more subsections until you arrive at the heading: *Dutch Painting*. Before you get to the bit about "the Sunday of life," Hegel says (I give it here just as I found it, in a translation published in 1920):

". . . And although its insistence on the insignificant and contingent includes the expression of what is boorish, rude, and common, yet these scenes are so permeated throughout with ingenuous lustiness and jollity, that it is not the common in its meanness and naughtiness so much as the gaiety and joviality which creates the artistic subject and its content. We do not look at mean feelings and passions, but simply at what is boorish, in the sense of being rustic, near to nature, in the poorer classes, a quality which connotes geniality, waggishness and comedy. In short, the Ideal itself is not wholly absent from the unperturbed easy-way-of-life."

Yes, here you really have a clue to the book.

People who have written considered studies on Queneau have said of *The Sunday of Life:* "Here, once again, philosophy and farce link hands across the page. The book's . . . central character . . . looks like a cross between the Good Soldier Schweik and Dostoevsky's Idiot, whom Queneau has called his favorite character in fiction." * "Again, the simple story of simple people conceals a philosophical theme." **

In contrast, one "quality" reviewer of the book when it recently appeared in England wrote: "The hero is good-natured to the point of stupidity, which doesn't prevent him from being pursued by a bawdy, middle-aged 'merceress' . . . who marries him. He is content enough, being fed up with the army and wanting a soft option. This is a strangely pointless novel . . ." All of which is strangely inaccurate: Julia is not bawdy (though her language sometimes is); Valentin is not in the least "looking for a soft option," and *The Sunday of Life*, far from being a pointless novel, has enough points to keep us guessing, thinking, musing, and chuckling for a good many months of Sundays.

(The same thing happens to most of Queneau's novels when reviewed in England. *Pierrot mon ami*, when it ap-

* Richard Mayne, "The Queneau Country," *Encounter,* June 1965.
** Martin Esslin, in *The Novelist as Philosopher,* edited by John Cruickshank, London, O.U.P., 1962.

peared in English in 1950, was described as "the kind of novel that is called 'so very French'; it is all very unassuming and amusing and most of us enjoy this kind of fun." But in books by people who had studied it a little more profoundly, it was called "One of Queneau's novels in which, from the beginning, the characters have a superabundance of wisdom," and Martin Esslin, in the book previously quoted, considers it "a book with a serious philosophy behind it . . . a poem on chance and destiny.")

So it seems that there is a fairly good case for an introduction to Queneau for the Anglo-Saxon reader. For instance, we may perhaps need to be helped to see why he chooses "boorish, rude and common" characters. Which he very often does. In his very first book, *Le Chiendent* (which *is* available in translation, as *The Bark Tree*), his chief characters are a junk-dealer, a café proprietor, a janitor, an NCO, a conjuror, a midwife, and a waitress. (The only intellectual amongst the whole bunch is there strictly as an observer.) In *Pierrot mon ami*, that "so very French" book, Pierrot is a vague young man who gets a vague job in a fairground because he doesn't know what else he could possibly do.

I think the reason for Queneau's choice of such characters is fairly simple. It is that, in common with an earlier, but equally unclassifiable and at times misunderstood writer, John Cowper Powys, he feels that the unpretentious man (or woman) in the street, "the common man," is potentially much more in touch with the realities of the world around him, and around us, than are the "experts," and that when the common man makes discoveries about life and about human nature he does it in an honest, straightforward way, and not in order to further his career, or his "image," or to get people to think how clever he is. Powys says that "the supreme masters are never professional philosophers," and goes on to maintain that "the further our great thinker advances in rational and esthetic elaboration, the more he loses touch with the magical fount from which his original inspiration sprang."

Queneau's humble characters remain in touch, and their discoveries about the world derive from simple curiosity, native wit, and love of life. Valentin and Julia are no saints—though at one point Valentin thinks it might be amusing to try to become one—but they are real, and they are interesting. They are also independent, and as free as they can be. When Valentin, at the end of the book, does actually start trying to be a practicing saint, this is basically only another of his individual ideas on how to pass the time. I suggested earlier that we didn't read novels just to "pass the time," but in a way the whole of *The Sunday of Life* could be taken as a meditation on precisely that subject. How *do* we spend our lives? Why do we do what we do? What does it all mean? Is it worthwhile? And what does it mean to say that something is "worthwhile"? Valentin, that "simple" character, tries literally to watch time passing, but he doesn't get very far. In this connection it is significant that Jean-Lackwit, who is taken by everybody else to be the district idiot, is precisely the person that Valentin chooses to discuss his philosophical ideas with.

Valentin and Julia are no saints, I said, but are they even really such simple characters? By the end of the book, we aren't so sure. The one person we are quite sure about is Valentin's brother-in-law, Paul. Queneau intends him to be such a nonindividual, so much the epitome of the man-on-the-make, whose only "values" are finance and prestige, that he gives Paul a new surname almost every time he appears. There are a good fifty varieties of his name, which starts and ends as Bolucra, and just occasionally he stops being Paul at all, and turns into Jules.

A vitally important element of Queneau's novels is the language he writes them in. From a very early age he was interested in language, from the one extreme of the language used in comic strips to the other extreme of linguistics. Two personal experiences crystallized this interest: the first was his military service in North Africa in 1925, and the other was some seven years later, on a visit to Greece. In North Africa he found that he didn't understand the ordinary language of the ordinary French soldier: when asked by a roommate: "est-ce que tu enlèves tes pompes?" he didn't know that he was being asked whether or not he intended to take his shoes off. And in Greece he became involved in discussions about the differences between classical and demotic Greek, and he drew his own analogies between the vitality of Greek and the ossification of French. "It was then that I saw it was obvious that modern written French must now finally free itself from the conventions that still hemmed it in; the conventions of style, spelling and vocabulary that date from the grammarians of the sixteenth century and the poets of the seventeenth."

This was a peculiarly French problem, Queneau saw, for as he said: "English writers write spoken English, and American writers write spoken American. And the most striking thing of all is that their scientists, their scholars and their historians write an English that is the English of the man in the street, whereas in France, when it comes to science or history, we are still obliged to write in formal language . . . French speakers are under the illusion that spoken French is slang, or imitation slang. But it isn't that at all. The thing is that people who think they express themselves in correct French don't do so in the least. They don't realize it, but they are using a syntax that isn't anything like what they are taught at school . . . I want to write in a living language—in the language of the ordinary man. The language you want to write in is your so-called maternal language."

And this is what Queneau did, right away, in his first novel, *The Bark Tree*. In his renovation of the French written language, in what he called a *third* French, a freewheeling creation somewhere between the old conventional written language and the actual spoken language, syntax, as he said in the quotation above, was not the only element which needed to have its cobwebs brushed away: there were also vocabulary and spelling. He has written quite a lot, and quite seriously, on the theoretical aspects of all this, but in his novels he presents it all with his dead-pan, take-it-or-leave-it humor. For he sees no reason why serious things should not be presented in a lighthearted or humorous way. Queneau is in love with language; one of the expressions of his love is the way he treats it as a living entity, and feels free to amuse himself with it, play around with it, renew it. James Joyce felt the same way. Queneau has said, by the way, that he acknowledges the influence of Anglo-Saxon writers, Joyce, Faulkner, and Conrad in particular, but not that of any French writers.

In amusing himself with language Queneau indulges in puns, invents new words, and sometimes, when he feels like it, spells words as they are pronounced, or runs a whole series of words together. Here again there is at least a semiserious purpose behind the fun. Why should spelling be so illogical?—he has often asked. And isn't it odd that people will, and do, sometimes pronounce a whole phrase as one word? Hence the famous first word of *Zazie dans le métro:* "Doukipudonktan," which stands for: "D'où qu'ils puent donc tant," which in itself is what the dictionaries call a pretty "familiar," or "vulgar," way of saying: "How come they stink so, though?"

In *The Sunday of Life* there is relatively little of all this word play, but there is nevertheless still quite a bit, thank goodness, and the book contains the word that you will find quoted in every discussion of Queneau's language, whether in English or in French: "Polocilacru." Meaning: "Paul aussi l'a cru." Meaning, (to us): "Paul believed it too." So this word simply had to be left intact in the translation—with a bit of explanation worked in.

In an interview Queneau gave to Marguerite Duras, one of her questions was: "Many people consider you the most serious novelist of our time. And others say: 'Heaven forbid that Queneau ever becomes serious! What do you think about it?'" Queneau's answer was: "I don't care either way. In *Zazie,* there is a moment when Gabriel is to some extent my spokesman. He has just finished his act in the nightclub. A lady says to him: 'You were so amusing!'—and he answers: 'Don't forget the art in it, though. It's not just amusing, it's also art.'"

We were very sad to learn, after this introduction was written, of the death of Raymond Queneau on October 25, 1976.

BARBARA WRIGHT

The characters of this novel being real, any resemblance they may bear to imaginary individuals must be purely fortuitous.

. . . it is the Sunday of life, which levels everything, and rejects everything bad; men gifted with such good humor cannot be fundamentally bad or base.

HEGEL.

I

LITTLE DID he guess, Private Brû, that every time he passed
her store the tradeswoman noticed him. He walked very
naturally, joyfully clad in khaki, his hair, what you could see of
it under his képi, his hair neatly cut and as you might say
glazed, his hands down along the seam of his pants, his
hands, one of which, the right one, kept rising at irregular in-
tervals to show respect to someone of superior rank or to answer the greeting of some demilitarized personage. Never sus-
pecting that an admiring eye was piercing him every day on
the route that led him from the barracks to the office, Private
Brû, who in general thought of nothing, but, when he did,
had a preference for the Battle of Jena, Private Brû moved
with unconscious ease. With his unconsciously gray-blue eyes,
his leggings gallantly and unconsciously wound, Private
Brû naïvely carried with him everything necessary to please a
maiden lady who was neither altogether young nor altogether
a maiden.

Julia pinched her sister Chantal's arm and said:

"There he is."

Lurking behind an amorphous clutter of buttons and spools
of thread, they watched him go by, without a word. Their silence was caused by the intensity of their examination. Had
they spoken, he would not have heard them.

As is his wont, Private Brû goes round the corner into the
rue Jules-Ferry and disappears for a little while. Until it's time
for chow.

"Well?" asks Julia.

"Well?" replies Chantal.

She goes and sits by the cash desk.

"Him?"

"There's thousands like that," says Chantal.

"And aren't there thousands like yours, too?"

1

"That's no argument."

"Well then, you see."

Julia continued to look languidly at the corner of the rue Jules-Ferry.

"What do I see?" asked Chantal.

Julia turned to her sister:

"It'll be him and no one else."

"Do what you like."

Chantal shrugged her shoulders and said, thus confirming her previous remark:

"Do what you like."

"Is that all you've got to say to me?"

If she gets married they'll have to whistle for her inheritance, the Bolucras, not for themselves, but for their daughter Marinette who might have, like, gone into the business, when her aunt began to, like, decrepitate. They'd find something else for Marinette. The Bulocras didn't need the auntly bazaar. They weren't chasing it. Let old Julia get hitched.

"You don't think he might be just a wee bit youngish for you?"

"How old would you say he was?"

"Twenty-two, twenty-three."

"You're seeing him in short pants."

"Twenty-five at the most."

She wasn't saying that, Chantal wasn't, to make her, Julia, back out. But she found the soldier a bit green for her sister who was so much less so.

"He's a good-looking man," said Julia, "he isn't a little boy."

"How wrong you are. He was born yesterday, your soldier. Squeeze his nose and cream'll come out. I say cream because I admit he's handsome."

Julia cackled.

"You'll always make me laugh."

"Not so much as you," said Chantal. "At this moment, *you* make *me* laugh, because you're going to make a hell of a mistake."

"How so?"

"Because you're going to marry a boy twenty or twenty-five years younger than yourself. Where's that going to lead you, eh? Just tell me: where's that going to lead you?"

2

She shook her hair coquettishly and answered her own question:

"Your marriage won't have a leg to stand on."

Julia faced her sister, then breasted her, and finally legged her. She asked her:

"D'you reckon I'm ugly?"

"No no, you've worn well. But a difference of twenty or twenty-five years, that's quite something. *You*'re old enough to have seen the French soldier-boys in their red pants marching past President Fallières.* *He* probably doesn't even know who President Fallières was."

"In the first place, thanks for the allusion."

"Have to say what is."

"And next, it isn't twenty years. And furthernext I don't give a damn. Answer me: d'you reckon I'm dilapidated?"

"Not at all."

"My puss?"

"All right."

"My boobs?"

"Bearing up."

"My gams?"

"Oak, eh."

"Well, then?"

"It isn't only people's physique that counts," said Chantal, "it's their morale."

"Oh, oh," said Julia, "where do you fish up such wisecraps?"

"Don't bother, I thought that one up myself."

"Come on, say what you mean, then."

Chantal then made allusion to men's habits, married men's, and in particular to those of her own, Paul Boulingra: obdurate alcoholism, autistic nicotinism, sexual sluggishness, financial mediocrity, sentimental obtuseness. Yes but the thing was, Julia considered that her sister had been singularly ill-served in the person of her Popol. She mentioned some fellows who drank nothing but water, like la Trendelino's husband, who didn't smoke, like la Foucolle's, who never stopped sweeping their chimney out for them, like la Panigère's, who earned a handsome living, like la Parpillon's,

* Asterisks in the text refer to notes on p. 179.

and who were capable of showing their wives the most delicate attentions, like the husband of the aforementioned M'ame Foucolle. Without counting the ones who could mend fuses, carry packages, drive the car, lower their eyes when they pass a hooker. Julia was fairly sure that her soldier would fall into the latter category, and this made her smile with pleasure. Which irritated Chantal.

"Yes," she conceded, "but when you're sixty, he'll be thirty-five. You won't keep him."

"We'll see."

"Then you're pretty clever."

"I shall manage."

"Do you think every man can be kept in the same way, stupid girl?"

"With him, I'll manage."

"You don't even know his name."

"So what?"

"You don't know his age, or his trade, or his past, or even if he's got his elementary school diploma."

"And what of it?"

"All right, my girl. All right."

Chantal tossed her hair femininely. She added once more: "All right."

Then she concluded:

"Carry on, then. Just carry on."

Julia finally sat down at the cash desk. There weren't any customers, she could, otherwise it isn't a good principle: the purchaser immediately thinks of the monetary consequences of his action and he doesn't buy anything. Better not to. So there she is behind the spring-actuated currency-harvester, a beautiful modern machine like they have in drugstores and in big cafés with orchestras and which, the machine, gave to Julia Julie Antoinette Segovia's modest commerce in threads and yarns, buttons and laces a serious and menacing appearance calculated to overcome the hesitations and indecisions of the buyers of gasoline-green ribbon or reddish-brown braid.

Julie took out a file, one for the bills, and started poring over the dates when they would fall due. She'd already done so seventy-seven times since the first, but once too often never does any harm. What was more, she wasn't even thinking about what she was doing. While her fingers were following with illiterate industry the signs that the West owes to the inventors of gum arabic, Julie was preparing a little speech destined for her sister with a view to some practical results. But Ganière came in.

Sent on various errands so as to leave the sisters to chew the fat in peace, the slave had gotten back to the store far sooner than was expected.

"They're all the same," said Julie to Chantal. "When you want them they're never there, and when you don't want them they come rushing back as fast as their legs'll carry them."

Ganière's zeal distressed Julie who measured, in the space of a few milliseconds, the distance that separates masters from servants, and especially the intelligence of the ones from the obtuseness of the others. The dope, she muttered, and then, in a curt voice, she pronounced these words:

"You certainly took your time!"

"But Madame," the girl began.

"That's enough," said Julie. "You've been hanging around street corners again."

"But Madame," bleat bleat.

"Yes, hanging around. Hanging around with bums. Or even with soldiers."

And yet she'd been quick, had Ganière. She would never understand.

"But Madame."

"That's enough. So you've been tumbled again, eh, you little slut? I shall tell your mother, and your poor grandmother. So young, and such a whore!"

Julie sighed:

"A veritable hetaera!"

She opened her mouth, but she had no time to protest. Julie leaned over toward this she, and the cash desk was high, and the hussy no more than knee-high to a duck. She trembled.

Julie got down from her chair, dived under a counter and pulled out a little package which she flung at Ganière.

"Go and deliver this, and get a move on."

"But Madame . . ."

"But what?"

"It's for M'ame Foucolle. She said she'd call for it."

"That any of your business?"

"Ida know, Madame."

"Then I tell you to go and deliver it. Your opinion is not of the slightest interest to me, my girl."

She bowed her head before setting out again for the streets of le Bouscat and, having bowed her head, did actually set out again for the streets of the said suburb.

Ganière gone, Julia climbed up onto her chair again and said:

"What a job you have to get anyone to do what you want."

"Don't talk to me about that," said Chantal, even though she only had a cleaning woman.

"So long as the government doesn't get into the act."

"Could be."

"Or maybe, it's because it does get into the act."

"Very likely."

"It's like the government employees."

"Oh, leave the government employees alone."

So Julie left the government employees alone, not so much on account of her brother-in-law, Paul Brelugat, inspector of weights and measures, as on account of her sister, Chantal Marie-Berthe Eléonore, wife of a certain Brolugat (Paul), whose labor and industry had led him, after much anguish, to the position of inspector of weights and measures in Bordeaux (Gironde). He had just been appointed to a job in Paris, in the fifteenth arrondissement, a splendid promotion, the pretext for quite a few blow-outs à la bordelaise, moistened with aïoli, bathed in fondue, irrigated with Chambertin. Out of affection for her sister, then, Julie dropped the subject of government employees, even though every time she thought about it, about the said subject, she got into a real state. Enough.

"Oh, personally, you know, government employees," she said.

"Vyou got anything else to say to me?" asked Chantal.

"Do you really think I'm making a mistake?"

But she didn't actually seem to be asking this question.

"There's nothing to say that you can," replied Chantal.

Her casual tone made Julia look up.

"Say what you mean."

"Well, what I mean, it's obvious."

"Obvious? What's obvious."

Chantal stood up.

"Got to go."

She went toward the door, but Julia didn't budge.

"Say what you mean," she said.

"Suppose he's married."

"He doesn't wear a wedding ring," Julia immediately replied.

"I don't want to offend you, but you might not be his type."

"I'll manage."

"A difference of twenty years, that counts."

"Tisn't twenty years."

"Bet it is."

"Is that all you can find to say to me?"

"Isn't that enough?"

Julia, for a few seconds, bent over her bills and then, abandoning them to their folder, slid off her chair and went over to her sister, speaking to her in these terms:

"I'm sad that you're going to live in the capital, I'm going to miss you, little sister."

"You've found someone else to keep you company."

"That doesn't replace a sister."

"Well no. Well no. A sister, that can't be replaced."

Her hair rippled softly over the slightly shabby collar of her suit. Chantal searched her handbag for the rouge, the pink, the powder, the paste, the cream, the stick, the puff, the brush.

"Too true: a sister can't be replaced. You're lucky, you are."

"So what, Paris is only Paris."

"Even so."

Julie sighed.

Chantal smeared a carmine unguent over her lips, licked them, and finally smiled.

"You'll come and see us," she said.

Julia smiled likewise.

"We'll go to the Folies-Bergère."

"And to the Casino de Paris."

"To the Eiffel Tower."

"I'll get giddy."

"And to Père-Lachaise."

"Where the famous dead are buried."

They began to get sentimental.

"Do you remember," said Julia to Chantal, "do you remember Broad Alley?"

"That was well named."

"Do you remember, when we used to come out of school?"

"Yes. You and Mireille Bacroix and Sophie Bergier, you used to lure the boys there and take their pants down. I used to watch you, I was too small."

"We used to scare hell out of them, the little cherubs. And the headmistress even congratulated us because we made them respect our sex."

They roared with laughter.

"And," Julia went on, "when you got engaged, and we made Mum believe that you'd been eating so many melons that you'd got the dropsy."

Crylaughing, Chantal added:

"Polocilacru," thus coining one of the most celebrated examples of queneautic logosymphysis, meaning: "Paul believed it too."

"What suckers people can be," concluded Julia.

They were beginning to recover their composure when Julia began again:

"And the healer we invented!"

More laughter.

"Yes but that way," said Julia, "you had a marriage without a protuberance."

"Oh la la," said Chantal. "Oh la la. Oh la la."

She had to sit down again.

Panting, she mopped up her tears.

"You'll always make me laugh," she stammered.

Cultivating the inheritance of her spinster sister was really too much of an endurance test. And hell, Marinette would just have to do the best she could, later on. And anyway, at the moment, Marinette was a pain in the neck. She'd never seen such a kid: always touching herself, perverse, phony, lying, hypocritical, thieving, the works.

"And do you remember," Julie went on, already laughing

at the big joke reposing in their common memory that she was once again about to conjure up.

Chantal interrupted her:

"Listen. Vgot to go. Tell me quickly what you were wanting to ask me."

Julie kissed her.

" 'Bye, love. And remember to tell me everything you find out about him."

II

"I don't know, Madame," said the colonel.

Madame Botugat adopted a heartbroken expression.

"But Captain Bordeille will certainly be able to tell you. I shall telephone him without delay."

"Don't I talk good," thought he to himself, while Madame Botegat stood up, telling herself that, in the French army, the officers didn't seem to know their men too well, and that this was greatly to be regretted, in all probability.

"My respects, Madame."

What the fuck could they be doing, these officers, if, not content with not knowing their men, they didn't even try to get to know women. This one, the colonel, just barely polite. Not the slightest sign of gallantry. Nothing.

Captain Bordeille was no better. He was extremely suspicious. As you came down the hierarchical scale, the recommendation of the director of weights and measures for Guyenne and Gascony to General Tom-Dick-and-Harry, in command of the Bordeaux area, gradually lost its prestige.

"What precisely is it that you wish to know, Madame?" asked Captain Bordeille, saying to himself: yes, but don't I talk good.

Wishing to make the most of this advantage, while his words were still fluttering halfway between him and the lady and before she could get one of her own in edgewise, he quickly resumed:

"I must straightaway admit, Madame, that I am extremely surprised that General Tom-Dick-and-Harry should have authorized the giving of the slightest piece of information of a military order to a person of the sex which is called weak, undeniably charming though it be."

Captain Bordeille paused for a moment's breath in order to think, for he naturally could not speak and think at the same time, in order to think that it must certainly have been this beautiful chick who had inspired in him the silken phrase whose cocoon he had just so laboriously unspun.

In the meantime Madame Botrula, having finally observed that the French army could still occasionally veer toward the gallant, decided to take the offensive. Having a great admiration for Joan of Arc, she readily chose her metaphors from within the martial range. For my sister, she said to herself, which made her giggle, but this subtle state of mind had no other exterior echo than a delightful smile which, like a live grenade, smashed into smithereens the barricade Captain Bordeille was attempting to build.

"Captain," said Chantal, "I assure you that General Tom-Dick-and-Harry declared that he would do everything to enable us, my sister and myself, to discover the identity of this soldier, as well as his pedigree, his service record, his medical record, and any other details liable to interest the family of his prospective fiancée."

Captain Bordeille considered that the dame didn't talk half badly either. Impressed, he scratched his head.

"Seeing that the general," he began.

"Yes, yes," Madame Bodruga ran on, "the general."

"Well, if the general."

"Precisely, the general."

"Seeing that the general," went on Captain Bordeille.

Chantal accentuated her smile, while telling herself what an old fossil he was.

The captain lowered his eyes and pretended to engage in

useful activity by fiddling about with some papers placed there no doubt for just such a purpose.

"Right," he said, without looking up.

It was idiotic but, sitting where she was, he couldn't see her legs.

"Right," he said again. "What's he called then, your fellow?"

"My future brother-in-law, you mean, Captain."

Bordeille couldn't prevent himself from darting a furtive glance at her, timid and admiring. A salty, spicy, sexy broad, and, to cap it all, educated. Not bad. But perhaps her ankles were a bit thick.

"Excuse me," he went on, awkwardly.

"Not at all, not at all," simpered Madame Botucla, who was pitying the poor nut for being so hollow.

"Well then. What's his name?"

"We don't know."

Captain Bordeille looked apprehensively at the visitor.

"Might it not be necessary to know it?" he suggested warily.

"But," said Chantal, "isn't that what you're here for?"

"To know it?"

"Yes. To know it."

Madame Broduga adopted a severe expression.

"Naturally," he murmured, "naturally, the roster is my department, but . . ."

"Which adds up to how many?"

"What? I beg your pardon?"

"I'm asking you how many men you have on your roster."

"Four thousand six hundred fifty-seven," said the captain at top speed.

"Then it can't be difficult to find one man out of four thousand odd."

"Six hundred fifty-seven."

"Odd."

There was a pause. Captain Bordeille took advantage of it to mop his brow. Chantal dropped her bag so that, as she picked it up, she could push her chair back far enough to give the guy a good view of the calves in front of him, i.e. her calves, Chantal's. The captain didn't even attempt to get up and plunge to her aid. He was content to look.

"Well?" asked Madame Brétoga.

"What does he look like, for instance? Can you describe him?"

He was feeling more confident because he had just had an idea, and as he hadn't even been looking for one he considered himself all the more meritorious. Madame Brotéga pretended to be thinking.

"Tall," she said, in the far-off voice of women reading the cards, "dark hair, regular features, dressed in khaki . . ."

"Interesting," murmured Captain Bordeille, "interesting."

He was trying to think of what he could ask next, but without success.

"Perhaps you'd like to know his rank?" asked Chantal.

"Precisely. That's it. What is his rank?"

"Private."

"Tt, tt. Now that's a pity. That's a pity."

"How so, Captain?"

"It's very widespread."

He sighed.

"We shall be obliged to make lengthy inquiries. Very lengthy inquiries."

Once again, without even trying, he had an idea:

"And really, you don't know anything else about him?"

"He goes along the rue Gambetta every day, turns the corner beyond the locksmith's and goes down the rue Jules-Ferry."

Captain Bordeille leaned back in his armchair, and his triumph gave him a pallid hue and an insipid air.

"He works, quite simply, in the office of the isolated colonial troops."

"That's just what I was going to tell you."

And, without pressing the point:

"Then who is he, this boy?"

"But Madame, I don't know! I don't know!"

He was trying to look sincerely regretful, but he didn't manage to convince Chantal of this, for she didn't believe in soldiers' despair, though she didn't know why, and, as she didn't want this pseudodepressive state to continue too long, she immediately suggested a solution to the problem, which the captain accepted without hesitation.

12

They crossed the parade ground, accompanied by the admiring whistles of the men on fatigue duty, at the height of erotic exaltation. Flattered, Chantal swung her hips while Captain Bordeille began to treat her to various remarks of the utmost gallantry. In the car taking them to the office of the isolated colonial troops he adopts a respectful and distant attitude. In the car taking them back from the office of the isolated colonial troops, which as it so happened was the same as the first, his behavior becomes tinged with a touch of satyrism, asking Madame Brétoga to feel the material of the pants beside her, i.e. his pants. They crossed the barracks square again, accompanied by the admiring whistles of the men on duty, whose lasciviousness never seemed to let up.

In his office, Captain Bordeille came back to the subject, which subject was called Valentin Brû. Chantal had immediately identified him among the pen-pushers in the depot. While he was looking through his documents the captain chatted gaily, animated by the healthy joy provoked by that activity.

"Brû . . . Brû . . . Odd name, isn't it?"

"How so?"

"Er . . . I don't know . . . All names are funny, in a certain sense . . ."

"Mine isn't."

"Of course; I wasn't referring to you. But mine, for instance . . ."

"Yours isn't, either."

"Really? You think so?"

He swelled with pride.

The pages went by.

"Brû . . . Brû . . . I can't find it . . ."

Then he manipulated some index cards.

The cards went by.

"Brû . . . Brû . . . I can't find it. . . ."

A top sergeant, called to the rescue, started leafing and carding.

"Brû . . . Brû . . . I can't find it, Sir . . ."

After which the top sergeant's sergeant neither leafed nor carded with any greater success.

"Brû . . . Brû . . . I can't find it, Sir."

13

Then it was the turn of the lowest rank in the whole office, a private. Very painstakingly he leafed and carded under the eyes of his superiors. He could not, either, find the name Brû.

Captain Bordeille dismissed his subordinates, calling them sons of bitches and show-offs, then, very much at his ease, he bowed to Madame Bodéga:

"Madame, all this is very simple; he doesn't appear on our roster; consequently, I cannot give you any information, but, in order to make up to you for your trouble, may I suggest that you come and sip a glass of port with me one day in my cozy little one-room bachelor apartment."

"Cosi fan tutte," said the educated Madame Butaga, absently. "But not respectable married women."

"Charming! Charming! Very neat! Very neat!"

In actual fact, he didn't think it all that brilliant but, well, he's trying to make a conquest. As for Chantal, she is anxious to accomplish correctly the mission with which her sister has entrusted her.

"How is that possible?" she asks automatically, absorbed in the plans of action she was trying to map out for herself.

"What would you say, for instance, to Saturday, at aperitif time? What civilians commonly call the witching hour?"

Captain Bordeille seemed overjoyed at having spouted with such distinction. Madame Brétaga automatically got out her engagement book, at the same time as she inquired:

"The which what? What time is that?"

"But five-fifteen, dear Madame."

It was his turn to inquire:

"Perhaps you haven't known many soldiers?"

"A few. After their military service."

She was still pondering the inquiries to be made, and wrote in her book the day and time of the rendezvous. All of a sudden, she remembered:

"Captain! You haven't answered my question."

"What question, dearest Madame?"

"I asked you a question just now and you didn't answer."

"I seem to remember fairly clearly that it was I who asked the last question. Which was: Perhaps you haven't known many soldiers?"

"And before that, what were we talking about?"

"About the witching hour, dearest lady."

"And before that?"

"About my little bachelor apartment. I described it to you. Don't you remember? I took the liberty of evoking its aromatic odor and I pictured to you the different objects comprising its furniture: the hat rack, the umbrella stand, the citron-wood table, the wicker chair, the bidet, the bread box and the divan as deep as the tomb."

"I don't remember."

She put her notebook back in her bag and stood up. She held out her hand to him:

"Good-by, Captain. And thank you for . . . Ah, now I've got it, I've remembered my question. It's very funny, don't you think, that we couldn't manage to remember? This is what I wanted to ask you: how is it possible that Valentin Brû doesn't appear on your roster?"

"How, dearest lady, do you expect me to know? If he did so appear, I might be able to tell you the reasons why he might not so appear, but, seeing that he doesn't so appear, I really cannot see how I could tell you the reasons why he might so appear."

"That's true," Chantal admitted.

III

SERGEANT BOURRELIER pushed open the door of the Café des Amis and went in, followed by Private Brû. They sat down at their usual place and, before they had opened their mouths, Didine brought them the green baize cloth, the gray cards, a Pernod for Arthur and Private Brû's *vin blanc gommé.** Arthur and Brû then played belote for a good hour and, as on all the other days, the sergeant won. Then they sipped their

15

aperitifs, very slowly, Brû all the more warily in that, ever since the colonies with their hepatic diseases and their sun-strokes, he was always afraid that a little too much alcohol might go to his head.

When they'd finished, they looked at each other with mu-tual liking and, as usual, the sergeant suggested:

"Another?"

"You really want one?"

"We'll play for the round."

They played, and once again Brû lost. The second glass he drank even more slowly than the first one. After having sucked in thirty drops he put it down and, without looking at his comrade, announced that he wasn't going to re-enlist.

"Have you really made up your mind?" asked Bourrelier.

"Not to re-enlist, yes."

"Tell me, then, what are you going to do in civilian life?"

"That's just it."

"You haven't got a trade, eh?"

"Well, no."

"So?"

"I thought about becoming a street sweeper."

"Not a lot of future in street sweeping. Specially with all the progress in mechanization."

"Even so, there'll always be the finicky bits: the little streets, the little corners, the difficult places. For example, if a car is parked, a machine can't do a thing, whereas I can al-ways fish around underneath it and it'll at least be cleaner. I believe there's still plenty of opportunity for hand sweeping."

"Maybe. But even so, there's much more of a future in being a mechanic."

"Don't know the first thing about it."

"You could re-enlist in the transport corps or the engineers, you'd come out with a good trade, like they say on the posters."

"I told you I didn't want to re-enlist."

Sergeant Bourrelier sighed:

"You'll never be able to support a wife and children with your street sweeping."

"I never said I wanted to support a wife and children."

"I suppose you'd rather your wife supported you?"

Brû looked up, highly surprised.

"Is that possible?"

Arthur roared with laughter. Then, becoming serious:

"I've even found you one."

"You have? One what?"

"Here, we'll have another. It's too funny."

"No thanks. That's enough for me."

"You can't refuse me that."

"Oh well."

They waited in silence for Didine to bring them their glasses, always a bit fuller when it came to the third round. The sergeant touched Brû's with his, saying:

"To your love life!"

"What's all this about?"

Private Brû said that to please Bourrelier, but it didn't really interest him.

"It's simple: you've clicked."

"Not possible," said Brû. "And who is it?"

He didn't give a good goddam, of course, but his buddy would have been offended if he hadn't asked any questions.

"You know the little notions store in the rue Gambetta, a bit before you turn into the rue Jules-Ferry, between the barracks and the office?"

"No."

"There's lots of ribbons, and buttons, odds and ends, in the window, like there are in the window of every haberdashery, I might go so far as to say."

"I don't know it."

"*I'd* noticed it."

"*I* hadn't."

"Well, never mind. You'll notice it now."

"Why should I notice it?"

"You'll see."

Private Brû adopted the position of the attentive, seated listener.

"Well, it's like this," Bourrelier began, "it's the woman who owns this store that's got eyes for you."

"Don't know her."

"You *will* know her."

"Why should I know her?"

The sergeant banged on the table:

"Are you or are you not going to let me speak?"

"But I'm listening, I'm listening."

Brû felt the *vin blanc gommé* going to his head.

"As I was saying, then," went on Bourrelier, "the woman has got it badly and she's got the idea she's going to marry you."

"How d'you know all this?"

"Her sister told me."

"Do you know her sister?"

"Oh shit, are you going to let me speak? or aren't you?"

Brû having shut his mouth, Bourrelier went on:

"Coming out of the office at lunch time, you turned right and I was on my way to the mess. I was just wondering what there'd be for chow, I was hoping there'd be tripe and aspara-gus tips, I was even telling myself, you know, that that'd make a change from artichoke hearts Soubise, it's funny, don't you think, it was just at the very moment when I was thinking, you know, that we were beginning to have had enough of artichoke hearts Soubise, five times last week, can you imagine, well at that very moment this dame accosts me, but really something you know, a knock-out, absolutely ter-rific. Hell, I say to myself, this is no time to be on the make, but that wasn't at all what she wanted. She started straight in talking about you, get it?"

Brû nodded slightly, to say that yes, he did get it.

"We went and had a drink and she asked me to tell her everything I knew about you and so I told her everything I knew about you."

"And what do you know about me?"

"Is he a decent guy, she asked me. He certainly is, I replied. How old is he, she asked me. Twenty-five, I replied. And then she asked me: Is he a regular? I replied: He's going to be discharged in a month. And I added: But he might well sign on again. Oh! she exclaimed, do please tell him, Sergeant, not to do anything so silly, because my sister's nuts about him, she's in earnest, he'll keep the store with her, they'll make a great success of it and later on they'll even be able to treat themselves to a house in the country. And then she scolded me and begged me to stop you going back into the army."

"And is that all you said about me?"

"Oh, that was enough for her. That you were reliable, not a drunk, especially that: not a drunk, that pleased her. That you were an orphan born in le Vésinet, you'd signed on for five years and you were just back from Madagascar. There. She was very pleased with that. Especially that you aren't a lush. That made a very good impression."

"Didn't she ask you whether I didn't have a girlfriend?"

Sergeant Bourrelier considered this.

"No," he said, "she didn't say a word on that subject."

This fact started them musing.

"You know," Private Brû went on, "it isn't usually the women who do that."

"Who do what?"

"Who check up on the men."

"Oh yes it is. The parents always make a few little inquiries. It's quite in order. And her parents, they're her sister, a really good-looking dame, that's all I can say, which I already have said. They've got a mother, too, but she lives in the big city. So it's her sister who takes care of the Intelligence Department."

"Even so, in general, it's always the man who takes the first steps."

"In Madagascar, maybe, but in France things have changed. Why shouldn't the girls chase the boys?"

"I don't know."

"In France, it's often the ladies who propose."

"It's official, then?"

"Just a moment. The sister's going to report to her sister all the dope she's gathered about you thanks to me, and if it seems all right to her the notions lady will come and see you. You haven't got any family, have you?"

"No. But even so, what about me," said Private Brû, lowering his eyes, "can't I make inquiries about her?"

"A little business, no one could refuse that. She's a property owner, your intended. You can take her with your eyes shut."

"That's just it. She might be hideous."

"Are you going to play hard to get? When you haven't

even got a trade. I was letting you go on just now. Street sweeper! That was all you could think of! And now you're going to get picky because you're being offered a thriving little business?"

"Yes but, just imagine, what if she didn't have any legs?"

"So what? In the first place, that's no uglier than anything else, and then, even so, her sister would have told me."

"I'd rather be sure."

"They won't blindfold you in City Hall."

Private Brû, with a thoughtful air, knocked back his third *vin blanc gommé*. His head was spinning a little.

"It's funny," he murmured.

"You're a lucky son of a bitch," Sergeant Bourrelier stated, giving him a great clout on the shoulder. "Just at the moment when you were going to be at loose ends, you're offered a nice little home. Nothing to grumble at, have you?"

Private Brû didn't answer.

"Now what's wrong?" said Bourrelier.

Brû hesitated a moment.

"Nothing," he said. "Nothing."

What was causing him grave anxiety was that he was going to have to return Bourrelier's round and, if he drank a fourth *vin blanc gommé*, it would make him drunk. Not only did custom demand that you returned drink for drink, but also when a man had just offered you a rich marriage, prepackaged, and, as you might say, on a platter, you had to demonstrate your gratitude, even at the risk of inebriety.

"Didine," he called.

"No no," said Bourrelier, "I'll take care of that. Only of the last one, though. Not the other two; you lost them."

"We'll have another."

"No, man, that's enough. I'd be late for mess and I don't want to miss the openers. Hell, there's potage Dubarry to start with and I'd hate to miss that. All my congratulations, once again. You lucky bastard."

Before he left he treated him to an energetic and friendly thump on the back, while Brû waited for his change.

"Have you won in the lottery?" asked Didine.

"Who, me? No. I never buy a ticket."

"I always buy a tenth part of one."

"And have you ever won?"

"You don't need to bother about me, Meussieu Brû. But why did Meussieu Bourrelier call you a lucky bastard?"

"Are you interested?"

"Yes, I'm as curious as a cat."

"Well then, I'm going to get married."

"Oh! What a pity."

"That's what you call a pity?"

"'Course it is. I won't see you any more."

"That wouldn't stop me coming."

"It won't be the same thing."

"Haven't got change for five francs, have you?"

He would willingly have left her a tip of a hundred sous instead of ten, but he had a vague feeling that such an extravagance would constitute a great lack of tact on his part.

"There's something a bit odd," said Bourrelier, who had come back, "I must tell you, it seems that your name doesn't appear on the garrison roster."

"That doesn't particularly surprise me," said Private Brû.

"Just thought I'd let you know," said Bourrelier. "So long, I'm in a rush."

"So long," said Private Brû. "Hey! how d'you know?"

"The dame told me. So long."

"Hey! do you know her name?"

"My goodness, no."

"And the other one?"

"Not hers, either. All you have to do is look at the name over the store when you go by. So long, I'm going to miss the potage Dubarry."

"So long," said Private Brû.

"Well, who are you going to marry then, Meussieu Brû?"

"How should I know," said Valentin placidly.

"That's the sort of thing people do know."

She stayed there, standing by him, at one side, eighteen years old, with all she'd learned at the Café des Amis.

"In theory," Valentin answered this time, "it's, uh, someone whose name I don't even know, that's true, I even forgot to ask what she's called, the person who has chosen me."

21

"Maybe she has a ridiculous first name," said Armandine.

He laughed with her. He'd finished drinking and paying, he sat there and didn't give any signs of being about to leave.

Didine sat down at his side. The café had emptied, the proprietor had gone down to the cellar to adulterate his drinks, and nicotinic, anisitic and vinitic odors were lingering on the ravaged wood of the tables. Brû examined the glass that contained his *vin blanc gommé*. The pipes in his head were beginning to feel a bit overheated, and his face expressed a total lack of expression.

"Is she a storekeeper?" asked Didine.

"Seems so. She wants to chase me and marry me."

"She must know you, then."

"Looks like it. Hm, that's another thing I forgot to ask Bourrelier."

"Even so, you must have *some* idea who she is."

"Yes. She runs a notions shop on the rue Gambetta, just before you get to the rue Jules-Ferry. That's the way I go from the barracks to the office, but I've never noticed."

"Oh la la," exclaimed Didine. "I know. It's Mademoiselle Segovia."

"Do you know her?"

"And how. Oh la la."

Brû smiled gently, and asked:

"What's the matter? Is it a catastrophe?"

Didine started, put her hand over her mouth and blushed.

"Come on, what is it?" asked Brû.

"I'm sorry. I don't want to say anything nasty about anyone. And I don't want to make fun of anyone, either."

"You haven't made fun of anyone, Didine, and you haven't said anything nasty about anyone."

"No, but I was going to."

"I'm not married to this Mademoiselle, what did you call her? yet."

"Segovia."

"That's Spanish."

"Dunno."

"Tell me everything you know."

"You won't be angry?"

"She makes inquiries about me, so I can make inquiries about her."

"Of course."

"Come on then, spit it out!"

"I don't dare."

"Oh, come on. Tell me."

"You're quite sure you won't be mad at me?"

"I swear."

"Well then . . ."

"Courage!"

"Well then, she's an old maid."

"And so what?"

"But I mean, a real old maid. Something like forty-five."

"That's pretty old."

"Well, hell, it's not exactly what you would call the first flush of youth."

"And then what?"

"I don't dare."

"Come on!"

"She isn't a real mademoiselle."

"What d'you mean?"

"Seems she was in love with a guy and he was killed in the war."

"Which one?"

"The one with the war memorials. Oh, it wasn't exactly yesterday. And ever since, she never wanted to get married."

"I'd have thought that was all rather sad," said Valentin.

"Too true."

"And what's she like? Do you know her by sight?"

"I should think I do. Every so often I go and buy little thisses and thats from her. She's funny, she comes out with terrible wisecraps, you'd never believe it of a storekeeper, even one that's not married, really spicy ones, just like you soldiers. I think she's a bit nutty, with all due respect, Meussieu Brû."

"That's not so terrible. But what does she look like?"

"I already told you. She isn't very young any more."

Brû looked at her.

"And you, you *are* young, eh?"

" 'Course I'm young. Want to see my birth certificate?"

"And when are *you* going to get married?"

"When pigs begin to fly."

"Some do."

"Look, Meussieu Brû, if you keep on with your funny jokes like that, Mademoiselle Segovia won't be able to resist you. Only you'll have to jazz them up a bit. Want another *vin blanc gommé,* Messieu Brû?"

"No thanks, I'm off."

"You're taking your time."

Brû smiled and stood up.

"So long, Didine. I'll be back."

"Could be, Meussieu Brû. Could be."

At the corner of the rue Gambetta he stopped, not knowing what to do. He had meant to go and dine at the Gourmets Fameux, but then he'd have had to pass the shop in question. Irresolute, he marked time, feeling extremely wretched. His *vins blancs gommés* hadn't given him the slightest courage. Finally, he turned on his heel. The proprietor of the Café des Amis was smoking on his doorstep; he waved to Valentin, who returned his greeting. A bit farther on there was the Restaurant du Belvédère Fleuri, but Brû didn't dare go in on account of the probable prices. Les Routiers was so noisy; he chose the Bifteck Comme Á Paris which would no doubt be a bit expensive, but it couldn't be helped. A day like to-day. Even so, when he's halfway through the door, he beats a retreat and goes off in the opposite direction. Once again he passes the Café des Amis, whose proprietor, still smoking, gives him a curious look. Brû waves to him and the proprietor answers him in a loud voice:

"Going to be a nice evening."

"Great," Valentin replies politely.

At the corner of the rue Gambetta he turned in the direction that led away from the notions shop, brushing against the pendant sausages of the butcher shop. With rapid step he goes down to the streetcar stop. He'd go without his dinner. Then he wandered aimlessly around Bordeaux. When it had got good and dark, he came back to the suburbs. He arrives within spitting distance of the store. It's closed. A feeble, yellowish light just makes it possible to see boxes of buttons scattered around rather than displayed, and rolls of ribbons somewhat uncertainly piled on top of one another.

On the right, there was a spool of white thread; on the left, one of black. Here and there, divers objects: knitting needles, bicycle clips, a little screwdriver for a sewing machine, garters, a printed scarf on which you could see Mont Saint-Michel. Being able to see it, Valentin saw it, and he thought that it was a place to have seen. All he knew of France was Roanne, Clermont-Ferrand, Marseilles—which is where you leave from when you're going to Madagascar; and Bordeaux—which is where you come back to. He had no memory of le Vésinet, from whose charms he had been snatched at the age of two, and he regretted this. One day he might even become a tourist. And then he'd go and see a few famous places and, naturally, the battlefield of Jena.

He moved back a couple of steps to read the inscription. He read it without difficulty; it was composed of the simple and single word: "mercerie." On the glass door he deciphered a name: Ja Segovia, followed by a flourish. What sort of feminine first name is there that begins with a j and ends with an a? Valentin couldn't think of one.

IV

"GOOD MORNING, Julia," said Paul as he came in.

He looked odd.

"Good morning, Paul," said Julia, kissing him.

Well, yes. Every time they saw each other, as the good brother-in-law and the good sister-in-law that they were, they mutually deposited a couple of smacking kisses on both cheeks. This operation, then, made it possible to hear four times over the same noise that Eureka suction-darts make when you pull them off the target. An identical custom preceded their leavetaking.

After she had wiped her left cheek, which Paul had moistened a bit too much, Julia asked him without any more ado what the fuck he'd come to her place for. Actually he'd come to stamp her measuring stick before he left.

"You bug me," said Julia. "You just did it three months ago."

"Is it still short?"

"Just the two centimeters I took out between the twenty-seventh and the twenty-ninth."

"Ah well," sighed Paul, taking a bag out of his briefcase.

"Why are you sighing?"

"When I've gone, you could easily be in for some trouble."

"How much?"

"Fifteen years hard labor, for instance."

Julia shrugged her shoulders.

"It's enough to make anyone wet themselves laughing, listening to you seriously," she said nonchalantly.

He was now writing out a certificate of correct weights and measures.

She watched him in silence.

"And aren't you ashamed?" she asked him, when he'd given her the paper.

He looked at her, taken aback.

"And it's fellows like you that get promoted to the capital," she added scornfully. "Poor France."

"I really can't think what you can have to reproach me for."

"Writing false certificates. But don't worry, I won't tell anyone."

She cackled.

Paul put his things back in his briefcase, very irresolute. He was annoyed that the conversation should have begun in this way. He had prepared his little speech, but not with such an introduction.

"And how's Marinette?" asked his sister-in-law.

"Very well. Thank you."

"Still as much of a bitch?"

"Oh look here, that's enough, that's enough."

And here he was, getting irritated. He'd mess up his sermon if he didn't deliver it in cold blood. But Julia didn't let him off the hook. She went on:

"What d'you mean, 'that's enough, that's enough'? You could be a bit more polite. I'm not going to shout it from the house-tops that you're an unscrupulous bureaucrat, am I? So when I ask you for news of *my* family, you might answer me with a bit more propriety. Primo. And segundo, you aren't really going to deny that Marinette is a little bitch, are you?"

"No, no. 'Course not. But it's not a question of that."

"What d'you mean, it's not a question of that? Seeing that it's Marinette I'm talking about, it has to be Marinette and no one else that's in question."

"Naturally."

"And anyway, it's not her fault, poor child. You bring her up so badly, so very badly, even. And then she's got the bad blood of the Brelogats in her. You only have to look at your degenerate ears. Ah! if only Chantal could have produced Marinette without letting our race be contaminated!"

"Okay. Marinette is a little bitch, the daughter of an unscrupulous bureaucrat, but *you* are an old maid past your prime and you're going to make a monumental mistake."

Julie cackled:

"You certainly took your time getting round to it! So that's what you were hatching. The moment you came in I guessed from the way your ears were flapping that you'd got some sort of dirty trick up your sleeve. I didn't have to ask myself what it could be. I saw you coming with your great big ears."

"Do you really want to marry this boy?"

"I do."

"No but! You must be off your rocker!"

"That's my business."

"A boy more than twenty years younger than you!"

"Didn't think I'd marry a has-been like you, did you?"

"A fellow who hasn't got a job, and who'll eat up all your bread."

"I'll watch it. Don't worry about me."

She put her hand on her cash register with a triumphant air.

"Well yes!" exclaimed Paul, "it's just as big a mistake as the day you spent all your savings on buying that instrument which was totally useless to you."

Every time he saw the cash register he flipped his lid. Thousands of francs that Marinette wouldn't get. He hated that bit of machinery, he had a great deal to say about that object, but he came back to his subject.

"An incompetent idiot who's been a soldier for five years and who comes out still a private!"

"Everyone isn't as ambitious as you."

"And who doesn't even appear on the roster!"

"They're just waiting for you to come and weigh and measure him."

"That's a stupid thing to say, that's got nothing to do with it."

"What's stupid is for you to go to so much trouble for nothing. Because, d'you hear me?"

She went over and looked defiantly at him.

"Do you hear me? I'm going to marry Valentin Brû, and no one's going to stop me. Not even him."

Paul retreated a couple of paces, stammering: "Not even him, not even him."

"What about your mother?" it occurred to him to ask, "what's she going to think?"

"I hardly imagine that my mother, who at the age of sixty-seven started living with a real bastard, can have anything against what I'm going to do."

"Have you told her?"

"If anyone asks you, imbecile, you're to answer, cretin, that you don't know anything about it, idiot."

"I shall write to old Ma Segovia myself."

"So what? As if we hadn't quarreled."

"Even so, she's your mother."

"So long as her gigolo's alive, she won't be my mother any more."

"You haven't got a heart!"

"And you haven't got any trump cards! I am impervious to your wisecraps."

"The menopause is muddling your mind."

"Mind your own business; which is mensuration, not menstruation, you poor dope."

"Think of Marinette!"

"All right, let's think about her!"

"Don't you remember?"

"Let's bring up the past!"

"Even so, you did promise her she'd inherit your business."

"Nuts!"

"You even told her she could come and work with you when she was fifteen."

"I don't think that would be good enough for the daughter of a government employee. Go into trade? Never!"

"Let's talk seriously."

"That's right: let's chat seriously."

"Did you promise, yes or no?"

"Yes. But I've changed my mind."

"That's convenient."

"That's the way it is."

Paul raised his arms, swearing to high heaven, lowered them again and declared that it was a calamity to have to deal with such an old crow. He stuck his briefcase under his arm and, before he left, tried out a few new arguments. He asserted that the boy was certainly a bad egg like all the colonial troops, opium smokers riddled with syphilis and beriberi, real Pernod sponges.

"Not true: he doesn't drink."

"That's what they all say. But they make up for it on the quiet."

"And what do you do on the quiet?"

"We're not talking about me."

"I suppose you haven't got a bottle of brandy tucked away in a drawer in your desk?"

The old cow. One of her customers must have told her. Pradelier's wife, probably. Hm, he'd send him a hell of a bill before he left. And his other subordinates, ditto. While he was preparing the plans for his vengeance, he naturally couldn't reply.

"You see," said Julia very calmly, "that's what you are: a forger and a boozer. And you expect me to listen to a comic like you? Nothing doing," she concluded, tapping her chin with the two first fingers of her right hand.

Paul Brétouillat considered for a few moments orientating

the discussion in the direction of philological questions. He couldn't agree to people using words in inexact meanings and it had taken a great effort of will power on his part to abstain from criticising the use his sister-in-law made, for instance, of the verb to chat instead of its cousins to talk or to speak. But finally the little ritornello that had been humming away inside him for the last few minutes, "not even him, not even him, not even him" caused him to opt for a more rapid retreat.

"Ah well!" he exclaimed, in a tone no less falsely irritated than hypocritically resigned, "do what you like. You'll have no one but yourself to blame."

"We are in entire agreement."

He looked at her with compassion, and wailed:

"Poor girl!"

"What a joker!" replied Julia, pulling his ear.

"Ouch!" said he.

They kissed each other on both cheeks.

"Adieu, Julia."

"Adieu, Paul."

"Wait a minute," said Julia, "I've got something for Marinette."

She went and got a package she had already wrapped.

"It's a little pair of panties in Dutch lace for her doll. So that she won't have lost everything," she added, laughing cordially.

"You're really too kind. She'll be so pleased."

"Don't apologize. You know, I'd never have been able to sell it, that little remnant of Dutch lace. But it's the genuine article, remember that."

"I tell you, you're really too kind."

They kissed each other once again on both cheeks.

"Adieu, Paul."

"Adieu, Julia."

And Bredéga left, jubilant; so jubilant that he was afraid it might be observed in his bearing.

"The jerk," said Julia to herself, watching him as he went, "he's going to lecture my soldier, and he thinks he's clever."

She guffawed, sure of herself, and went back into her shop, ejaculating more than once "what a slut, what a slut," with reference to Ganière, whose absence, now that she has got rid of her brother-in-law, she finds unduly prolonged.

"Morning, Msieu," says Ganière to Brodouga, as she passes him at the corner of the rue Jules-Ferry.

"Evening, dear," replies Paul absent-mindedly.

He automatically looks back to squint at the kid's impoverished calves and then turns in the direction of the depot of the isolated colonial troops. It's ten forty-three. He sends word to Private Brû that a meussieu will be waiting for him at the gate at eleven o'clock. It's very important. Next he examines the neighboring bars and chooses the Café des Amis.

A pretty young girl pours out his brandy, but he doesn't notice her, he's so pleased. At the very moment when his promotion to the capital had come to recompense his work which had, indeed, been real, and above all subterranean, to which in any case Chantal had energetically contributed, it would really have been the bad luck of all time to let a filthy little adventurer get his mitts on old Julia's loot. Paul smiled to himself, he was so enchanted with the envisaged conversation, so much so that he wasn't even bothering to prepare it. But suddenly, his throat went dry. Hell! he hadn't thought of that: in a month's time he was going to leave Bordeaux, and Julia would be on her own. He had no doubt that he would obtain what he intended to obtain today, but a month from now he wouldn't be there to supervise its execution and success. Even if he managed to persuade the fellow to sign up for another five years, there was nothing to say that, unsupervised, Julia wouldn't marry the bloodsucker in question.

This discovery nearly made him cry. He had a second brandy, then a third, but his despair didn't abate. With the fourth, eleven o'clock struck. He paid rapidly, abandoning in his wake the minimum tip, and rushed over to the gate of the depot. Men were coming out. One of them was looking around him. That must be Brû. A handsome lad, he had to admit. Martial was the appropriate epithet. This lexicological success gave Botucat renewed courage.

"Meussieu Brû?"

This was asked politely, but without exaggeration.

"Yes, that's me. Was it you that was looking for me?"

Another innocent. Probably a habitual user of the pleonasm and the truism.

"Myself in person."

A bit too patronizing. Must go on in a lower key:

"My name is Jules Bodrugat."

Mustn't leave him time to look like someone who's trying to remember a name but can't. Add immediately:

"I'm your fiancée's brother-in-law."

It's done.

Paul holds out his hand to the soldier. The soldier doesn't hold out his hand to Paul.

"But I don't have a fiancée, Meussieu."

He has spoken in a simple, neutral tone that Brocula envies him. So Paul explains:

"I mean, I'm the husband of the lady you saw yesterday."

"What lady?"

Paul becomes irritated:

"The lady who came to talk to you about a possible marriage to Mademoiselle Segovia."

"Quite so," says Valentin.

He remains silent for a moment, looking somewhat tense, then adds:

"I know."

"Well then, my dear Meussieu Brû, I should be very glad to have a conversation with you."

Private Brû remains as reserved as before.

"The thing is, I've got to go and eat."

"You must realize that I wouldn't be troubling you if it weren't very important."

"All right then."

He puts his hands to his mouth and shouts to a buddy who's already at the end of the street to save a plate of food for him. Then, Brodoga and he agreed to hold the above-mentioned conversation over a glass of something and they go and sit in the Café des Amis.

"What will you have?" asks Paul, once again a little too cordially.

"A *vin blanc gommé*."

"And for Meussieu," adds Didine, "a brandy as usual."

Private Brû looks at him. He's never seen him here. And yet the guy's ears are of an exceptional size. He probably doesn't come at the same time as the soldiers. Brû, pleased to have thought of this right away, smiles amiably at Paul, who smiles back no less amiably because the waitress's remark has totally thrown him and because he also realizes that he hasn't in any way prepared his attack: he has come here in disarray. Neither opens his mouth until the drinks have been served.

"Your very good health," says Brodouillat, raising his glass up to his nose.

After which he lowers it slightly and sinks its contents at one gulp.

"And yours," replies Valentin.

He dips his lips into his *vin blanc gommé*.

Paul watches him: he isn't taken in. The fellow's putting on an act.

"Tisn't very good, eh?" he says, with a conspiratorial air. "Tisn't as good as Pernod, is it?"

Valentin makes a face, shrugs his shoulders vaguely and says, looking at his interlocutor's fascinating ears:

"That's what's going to please Mademoiselle Segovia the most, when she hears . . ."

"When she hears what?"

"That I'm not overfond of aperitifs."

"Of course. Of course."

"It was your good lady who told me that."

He's embarrassed by that look, which makes his ears burn and which he can't manage to intercept with his own, which is greatly overmoistened by all the brandies he has drunk that morning. He's confused, and a hair in his nostril is tickling him; he tries awkwardly to extract it. Valentin presses the point:

"And it isn't only aperitifs that I'm not overfond of," he adds, "but spirits as well. For instance, you'd have to pay me to drink brandy before a meal. And even after one, it's pretty rare."

He once again pretends to be thinking, and concludes:

"You might almost say never."

And he transfers his examination from the ears to the nostrils. Paul considers that really this bastard is going too far, he's a real son of a bitch, he's putting me on, but I'll get him, the bastard. You pig, you. You pig.

But suddenly, by good fortune, out of his joke reservoir there emerges a witticism which he had concocted when he was just about entering the age of puberty and whose freshness still charms him: "Sir, some cordial!" says he to himself, then. And, delighted, he resumes the conversation:

"Well, so it seems you saw active service in Madagascar?"

"Yes. Against the Merina Hain-Tenys."*

"It was tough, eh?"

"So-so."

"And Madagascar, it must be beautiful."

"Not bad. Rather mountainous."

"And the natives?"

"Well—no shortage of them."

"Ah! travel, it's nice to travel, and it broadens the mind."

"Yes, I'd like that: to travel."

"You've got nothing to complain about!" exclaimed Bredouillat with servile cordiality.

"I'm not complaining," protested Valentin.

"And what would you like to see, soldier?"

"Jena," replied Valentin without hesitation.

"What?"

"Jena. The battlefield of Jena."

"In Germany?" asked Paul, scared.

"Do you know it?"

"I must admit," said Paul, smiling like a coward, "that the idea has never entered my head . . ."

"Oh!" Valentin interrupted, "there are things to see in France too: Mont Saint-Michel, the Eiffel Tower, Mont Blanc."

"You like high places," said Paul, with a stupid little laugh that he couldn't control. "Whereas Julia my sister-in-law, Mademoiselle Segovia, that is, she can't bear them."

His confusion was such that, at one stroke, he had got back to the subject under discussion. Carried away by his own impetus he threw himself on the hand Valentin was advancing to pick up his glass and kneaded it between his own, stammering, with tears in his eyes:

34

"Don't marry her, soldier. Don't marry my sister-in-law. It's disinterested advice I'm giving you, it's a brother-in-law speaking, it's the solemn entreaty of the father of a family, it's a desperate adjuration, it isn't a load of crap, it's the bona-fidiest of all possible bona-fides. Don't marry her, soldier. Don't marry her."

He was sniveling. Valentin went back to his examination of the guy's ears: surely, all the fellow had to do was flap them and he'd be able to fly. Looking up, he met Didine's eyes; he winked at her and, while Bradégat was dabbing at his tears, he raised his right hand to his temple and repeatedly rotated its index finger.

V

It was all plain sailing, however. Three months later they were married, ex-Private Brû and Mademoiselle Segovia. Afterward, there was something that was indispensable but, well, there you are, it was already October: couldn't possibly close the store in the busy season. They discussed it at length, ex-Private Brû and the notions lady. Had to face reality: in fact, hordes of customers were throwing themselves onto the pearl buttons, the braid, and the adhesive tape: they weren't so rich that they could afford to miss all this good business.

No, of course not, said Valentin. You see, then, said Julia. And yet, said Valentin, and yet, it's obligatory, a honeymoon. In theory, said Julia, in theory mnot saying it's not. You see, then, said Valentin. Have to admit, said Julia, have to admit that a marriage without a honeymoon, that doesn't exist. No, said Valentin, no, that doesn't exist. Yes, said Julia, yes but the busy season is the busy season, and there's no changing the seasons. Maybe we could put the honeymoon off until our next vacation, suggested Valentin. And when will we take the vacation, then? Julia objected. And he had no answer to that.

They ended up by adopting the only possible solution, the one and only, to wit that Valentin alone would go on the honeymoon alone. During which time Julia would continue to make the wheels of commerce turn and would pile up the shekels. Having agreed on the principle, they went on to determine the duration: two weeks seemed enough. You get tired of too much intimacy, and in the long-run dalliance, nothing but dalliance, becomes wearying: two weeks, just long enough to get the taste without the distaste. Then they decided on the target: keeping the battlefield of Jena for a later date, Valentin suggested Mont Saint-Michel, but Julia preferred Bruges, Bruges-la-Morte in Belgium, not the Bruges a couple of kilometers away from le Bouscat, down by the marshes. Touched by this choice, which seemed to him a delicate compliment to his last name, Valentin comes round to this suggestion. All that's left now is to decide on the itinerary: naturally one will go via Paris, twenty-four hours in the capital, that's always a pleasure, one of those memories you don't easily forget. No point in going to the Brébagras, who've hardly had time to settle in: one would disturb them and anyway one had one's whole life in front of one to see them. No, but one would make a beeline for the Folies-Bergère. This project Valentin finds less attractive. It's incredible, so they say, how easy it is to get lost in Paris. What's more, you get yourself run over, pickpocketed, and busted. Plenty of trouble ahead, thinks ex-Private Brû, but he didn't dare thwart such a legitimate desire. Since he had to spend an evening at the Folies-Bergère, very well then, he would spend it. And everything was thus amicably agreed.

Julie went with him to the train, she'd reserved him a third-class window seat, she hadn't specified that it should be facing the engine because it was all the same to her: she wasn't one of those women who suffer from nausea as a result of minor details of that sort. She got into the car with Valentin, a lovely car with a corridor running the whole length of all the compartments, with at either end sumptuous double-you-sees, the use of which Julia recommended to Valentin. Then, on her advice, he put his hat on his seat to keep his place, and also a vaguely licentious publication that she had bought for him with this end in view. You could never be too careful, she said, darting ferocious looks about her, there's always bastards who come and take seats they're not entitled to. There's even some, adds Julie, who pull off the reservation stubs. That's disgusting, don't you think, Mesdames?

She was addressing her remarks to the only two occupants of the compartment, two peasant women sitting primly on the edge of the only two unreserved seats. The other tenants, sure of their rights, were in no great hurry. As for Valentin, he had managed to arrive at the station twenty-five minutes early. And he had also just managed to shove up into the baggage-rack a heavy, aluminium-encased contraption, a chest he'd brought back from the colonies and which would do him for a suitcase. Julia had a nice one for vacations, but they wouldn't expose that to wear and tear on this occasion. Valentin, delighted with his success, turned back to Julia.

"That's lousy," she was saying to one of the peasant women, fingering her scarf. "Rotten quality. I bet you bought it from a peddler, didn't you?"

The woman smiled in admiration, amazed by so much perspicacity.

"If you want something really first class, that'll last you all your life, come and see me, then: Mademoiselle Julia, rue Gambetta, in le Bouscat. I'll give you something off."

"Thank you very much, Madame."

"Coming?" she asked Valentin. "We can't hang around here till it leaves."

She turned to the female hayseeds and called out:

"Keep his seat for him! Hm?"

"Yes of course, Madame. You can rely on us, Madame, you can rely on us."

On the platform, they looked at the train, a beautiful express.

"It's great to travel," said Julia. "I reckon there's nothing like travel, it's much better than the movies. Anyway, most of the time the movies are for halfwits. Don't you think?"

"Yes," said Valentin.

She looked at him.

"You don't look particularly cheerful," she remarked.

He didn't answer immediately, he was hesitating between three equally true propositions: "I do feel cheerful, but it's not obvious," "I'm not so specially, because you aren't coming with me," and "I'm afraid someone's going to swipe my seat."

"I'm talking to you," said Julia. "You're not with me. Where are you? In the moon? I said: you don't look particularly cheerful."

"Who, me?"

"Yes, you. Obviously you. Not the guy next door."

And, addressing her remark to a meussieu who was listening, all the time pretending he wasn't:

"No, no, Messieu, mnot talking to you, mtalking to my lambkin."

The guy went his way.

"Well," Valentin began.

Julia interrupted him.

"Don't talk rubbish, and have a good time. Do you have your money?"

"Yes, I do."

"Don't let anyone rip you off. You've got enough for a fortnight, you'll see. Obviously, when you're in Paris it'd be better not to eat chez Drouant."*

"Yes, better not."

"And you're going to send me post cards, don't forget."

"No, I won't forget."

They walked up and down along the train. The dining car aroused their admiration.

"Have to treat ourselves to that, one day," said Valentin vaguely.

"Seems their food's terrible," said Julia. "It can't touch a nice picnic basket packed at home."

"No, of course not," said Valentin.

He noticed that he hadn't got one with him, a picnic basket packed at home. But he wasn't hungry.

"There's quite a crowd," Julie observed. "You'd better get back to your seat."

They kissed.

There were some people standing in the corridor. In spite

of his fear of irritating them, Valentin thought it possible to disturb them. In his compartment, his corner seat was still vacant; the peasant women had valiantly defended it. All the other seats were now occupied. His hat was a problem; Valentin resolved it by putting it, the problem, on his head. He looked toward the platform, to wave his handkerchief, but he didn't need to get it out. Julia's back was already disappearing.

So he starts to study his supposedly amusing paper. On its cover he sees a partially unclothed young woman who is stroking the beard of a marble faun. Valentin attentively studies this bonbon-colored picture and, in conformity with the desires of both the artist and the editor of the magazine, he thinks that the naked young woman is the possessor of undeniable charms. He particularly admires her contours, and passes a curious index finger over them. But the reproduction is flat: the ass is an artistic effect. Valentin sneaks a look around him: the two peasant women are watching him with tender emotion, but a big fat meussieu gives him a severe glance. Valentin hurriedly turns the page. To judge by the stationary platform, we're still in Bordeaux.

Valentin starts reading the next page: there people are recommending contraceptives, genuine marriages, methods for increasing your stature or defending yourself in the street. The other two pages expatiate on the same questions, and some colonial troops are looking for lady pen-friends, otherwise known as godmothers. In Madagascar some of his buddies used to amuse themselves in this pursuit and when they went home on leave they had it made, so they said. Not understanding that writing might serve to transmit inexactitudes, Valentin hadn't even tried. He glanced around him once more. This time the train had actually started. Some engines were parked in a semicircle and various sanitary operatives were cleaning express trains that had served their purpose. The number of tracks diminished, the express chose its own, and began to travel along it with rapidity and resolution. The train was moving. Satisfied with this observation, Valentin went back to the examination of his magazine. At the top of page five there was a drawing. Valentin examined it; it showed two lines of haggard personages, poorly and archaically dressed. The caption explained: "Cenobite community members sadly lack exercise," which plunged Valentin into the extremes of stupefaction. Even though he had, during the course of his sojourn in Diégo-Suarez, read, from the first page to the last, not forgetting the pink ones, the *petit dictionnaire Larousse français et encyclopédique*, which had opened in him the floodgates of knowledge, he didn't feel sufficiently confident in his knowledge of the meaning of the word cenobite to find the suggested image funny. Perhaps the fat meussieu sitting opposite him would be able to explain it to him; if so, that would enable him, after they'd had a good laugh together, to ask him whether this was actually the Paris express.

Good Lord, Valentin silently exclaimed, in fact that's true, am I on the right train for Paris? He looked at the landscape: the flowing greenery gave him no information. He turned back toward his companions: the fat meussieu was still keeping him under unbenevolent observation. He'd never dare. The peasant women were sausaging. As for the other people, each one had already built his own barricade. Valentin wondered what to do; somewhere on the train there must be an employee qualified to tell him, even if it were only the engineer, but how to find him? He'd have to go out of the compartment, disturbing the peasant women's snack and revolting the people in the corridor, all things which Valentin felt incapable of doing. He was perhaps beginning to feel a little unhappy when he thought he remembered that they stopped several times before Paris; if he'd made a mistake all he had to do, then, was to get out at the next station; if he was in fact on the Paris line he could simply take the next train. In this way he wouldn't annoy anyone. He pulled his hat down over his eyes and fell asleep immediately.

The fat man was buying a sangwidge and a can of beer from someone down below. Valentin jumped. He made a grab at his trunk and, pulling it unabashed over the other travelers' knees, soon found himself at the station exit. He handed his ticket to the employee face downward, fearing that he might be asked for an explanation; for, at all events, this was certainly not Paris. He was afraid he might look like a dope or a malefactor, getting out like that no matter where.

He would willingly have taken to his heels when he was called back, but his luggage prevented him attempting any sort of performance. He retraced his steps and learnt with lively interest that he could keep his ticket, which was still valid for the journey to Paris. The employee's benevolence seemed to him so great that he wasn't afraid to abuse it by inquiring about the time of the next train for that town, which question was answered with exemplary precision. Could he once again take advantage of such kindness? He confides to his new friend that he has heard tell of a place, located in stations, where one might deposit packages, suitcases, or knapsacks without entertaining any fears that anyone might appropriate them, since the administrative services of the railroads graciously undertook to supervise them, and this against a moderate charge.

I must be inconveniencing him, thought Valentin, seeing the strange look that came over the guy's face. With his thumb, the latter pushed his emblazoned cap slightly backward in order to examine this traveler more attentively; after a silence of some three seconds, he returned his headgear to its place and indicated the way to the baggage checkroom in some detail.

"A thousand thanks," replied Valentin, delighted with the agreeable turn that events were taking.

He thought it appropriate to embellish this acknowledgment, which was perhaps a little perfunctory, with a witticism which might pour onto their uniquely administrative relations a little of the milk of human kindness.

"And pardon me if I excuse myself!" he shot at the man of stations, with a pleasant smile.

The man of stations could not conceal his extreme surprise.

VI

AFTER HAVING wandered round the streets of Angoulême, exceptionally deserted that day, he recovered his suitcase with amused astonishment and, on the stroke of four in the morning, got into a semiexpress train which often doubled as a local. A compartment was empty; he fell asleep in it, happy.

Later he had some fellow travelers, but they turned out to be ephemeral, not, in general, going in for trips of more than four or five stations. As they changed, they enabled him to observe at the same time the variety and the uniformity of the French population and, as this was now his second journey in less than twenty-four hours, he felt very much at his ease, he even felt slightly protective toward the most hayseedish of them. But, as they got near Paris, he regained his modesty.

At the Gare d'Austerlitz, he lets himself be swept along by an avalanche of people so enormous that you would never have believed that the train could have contained so many, and who seemed to know precisely what to do. When he finds himself faced with an automatically shutting subway gate of the metro, Valentin steps back, terror-stricken. He's going to get lost. You always get lost in the metro. He turns round, sticking the metallic corners of his overnight case into the rotulian region of the nervous types, ever ready with the starting insult. He heard himself designated in very strange ways and felt ashamed, exactly what the nasty fellows intended. After having perturbed the marvelous circulatory order of the Parisian vaults, he finds himself on a sidewalk again. He puts down his wardrobe and sits on it.

It was five o'clock in October. People were walking every which way and, on the avenue, circulating in every direction. An anarchistic agitation caused beasts, engines, and people to stir spasmodically, and they all accompanied their disorder by sounds which in general were ear-splitting. A bearded blind man was playing the flute with his nose, interweaving into the thread of his meager melody the squawkings and screechings of men and things on their way.

The evening papers were being hawked with such frenzy and energy that Valentin thought war had been declared. That would certainly come one day, though. Today, it would be the last straw. But no, it couldn't be war, otherwise it'd be the bugle that the blind man would be playing.

He couldn't stay there. In spite of their haste, people were sparing time to glance at him. Maybe he was going to cause an unlawful assembly, an offence under the Riot Act. He got to his feet and, picking up his trunk with an energetic arm, undertook the continuance of his journey. In a few steps he was by a river, probably the Seine; and he perceived a campanile adorned with a vast clock which seemed to him to belong to a station and, with any luck, to the station called the Gare du Nord.

As this luck was not vouchsafed to him he took to the road again and, as six o'clock was striking, arrived at the Place d'Italie, which was enlivened by a fair. He stops for a moment to admire the beautiful disposition of the monuments surrounding this intersection and then, tireless and courageous, he marches with confident step toward the Porte de Châtillon where, sure enough, he reports forty-five minutes later. Judging from the width of the carriageway that he must finally have got to the *grands boulevards,* fearing on the other hand to miss a train the time of whose departure he is unaware of, exhausted by the transportation of his luggage and by hunger, not having known how to lunch during his journey, he decides to take a taxi which can't possibly cost very much, because he thinks he must have covered at least three quarters of the distance on foot. But, contrary to what he thought, the said distance turned out to be extremely long, and even longer since the taxi driver went round by the Porte de la Muette and the rue Caulaincourt. What bothered Valentin the most was all the time he was making this good fellow waste, when he would no doubt have preferred shorter and easier trips.

At the Gare du Nord Valentin extirpated his suitcase and looked at the meter; he couldn't believe his eyes, and this to such a point that he formulates it to himself in this manner: "I can't believe my eyes."

"That was a long way," he said to the driver.

"I should say," replied the other.

"Wait for me," Valentin added quickly. "I'll just go and put this thing in the checkroom and then you can take me to the Casino de Paris."

"It's a bit early to go there," remarked the taxi driver in an access of sincerity.

But, seeing the disconcerted expression on his client's face, he hastened to rectify:

"But you need to be there early if you want to get seats."

While the taxicrat was wondering whether he'd go round by the Avenue de Reuilly or the Boulevard Victor, Valentin, made confident by his adventure in Angoulême, after having experienced once again the joy that every traveler feels when he entrusts his luggage for a certain time to honest, orderly public servants, Valentin inquired seven times over at seven different windows the time of the train for Bruges. The replies tallied. He nevertheless proceeded to a verification by consulting the yellow notice boards placed at the disposal of the public. Having managed to convince himself that there was every possibility that he might effectuate his departure on the stroke of zero hours seventeen, he finally makes his way over to a door on which someone had written "Exit." It gave on to a dark little street ending in a stairway, which Valentin doesn't hesitate to take. At the top of this stairway he turns left, haphazard. Fairly rapidly, he finds himself in front of the station again. It looked quite different than it had just now; he goes in and doesn't recognize the order of the ticket windows, nor the architecture of the tobacco and candy stands. A vast fresco representing the departure of the troops for the 1914 war informs Valentin that he is at the Gare de l'Est. He admires the work of art in detail at the same time as he reflects that they'll soon have to make another, another work of art, for the coming one, the coming war, because it was no use counting on getting out of it, the coming other one.

Saddened by these considerations, he left this faintly lugubrious spot by way of a door on which someone had written "Entrance," since the previous time the exit one had led him astray. He congratulated himself on his decision, for he perceived in front of him a magnificent boulevard punctuated with lights. Numerous and sumptuous brasseries offered to the passers-by the charm of their terraces or the luxuriance of their wall sofas. As he hadn't had anything to eat for twenty-four hours, Valentin decided to treat himself to some dinner. After having walked eight times past each of the six establishments in the neighborhood, and each time having read the menu from the first to the last line, he opted for a tavern which seemed to him to combine comfort with reasonable prices. In between times he purchased four post cards and a corresponding number of stamps.

"Well," said he to the waiter, with a winning air, "what's today's specialty?"

I'm learning, he thought, with some satisfaction.

"Zthe *plat du jour*," replied the waiter, studying, out of pure curiosity, a molding on the ceiling.

"Tsava look," said Valentin.

Hell, where was it, the bloody *plat du jour*, he couldn't track it down.

Having lowered his eyes, the waiter discovered his customer's distress.

"On the other side," he articulated scornfully. "The menu at seven francs fifty."

Valentin, having obeyed, and reversed the bit of pasteboard, discovered that for this sum, which was not beyond the limit of his means, it was suggested that he might consume some salami, a pork chop with fresh haricot beans, some gruyère cheese, and some apple sauce. He was even offered a quarter of a bottle of red wine. A violent joy entered his heart and made him salivate. There was only one slight shadow on his happiness, but given the supremely elegant way in which the waiter chucked his knife and fork in front of him, plus the basket with the bread cut into slices, he didn't dare ask him, the said waiter, what sort of activity might be indulged in by a taxi driver whose fare doesn't come back to pay him. This ignorance didn't prevent him from doing justice to the entire meal, even unto and including the skin of the salami and the rind of the gruyère. Finally, having cleaned up the remotest corners of the rather fancy receptacle in which his apple sauce had been produced, from one pocket he pulled out a pencil, and from the other his post cards. They all portrayed the Gare de l'Est.

He chose the one that was the least soiled to send to Julia. After having licked the point of his pencil, he wrote straight off and without hesitation: *From Paris without you, your beloved husband,* and the signature: *Valentin.* Then he consulted a bit of paper for the address, because he still didn't know it by heart. Without pausing for breath he immediately started on the second post card, and without much difficulty these words occurred to him: *With best wishes from the capital, your new brother-in-law,* and the signature: *Valentin.* The same bit of paper previously consulted informed him of the address of the Bratagas. For the third post card, all he could think of was: *Hallo from Panam, your buddy,* and the signature: *Valentin.* This was for Bourrelier. On the fourth postcard, destined for Didine, Valentin wrote: *Guess who,* and didn't sign it. Having stuck on the stamps, he put the four communications in his pocket.

The payment of the bill passed off without difficulty. He left a tip which seemed to give the waiter entire satisfaction and, happy not to have displeased this individual, Valentin, having consulted the turnip watch that Julia had given him for his wedding, estimated that he had plenty of time to go for a little walk before trying to find the Gare du Nord again.

At a first glance, he decided that on the whole the stores aren't too bad, though nothing like so sumptuous as the ones in the Cours de l'Intendance, in Bordeaux. The first that caught his eye sold radio sets. Valentin told himself that it would no doubt please Julia to have a contraption like that, which made a noise all the year round. She'd even be delighted. He looked at the prices, they seemed to him very high. Having observed that fortunately the store was shut, he thought how happy Julia would be when she heard that he hadn't wasted any money on buying an instrument that does nothing but talk crap. Enchanted at having given his wife this little joy, he was about to continue on his way when he noticed that a young person at his side was looking at him and smiling. After he had made sure by means of a circular glance that this smile was indeed intended for him, he raised his hat politely and in these terms expressed himself:

"I apologize, Mademoiselle, for not recognizing you. I hope you aren't offended."

Disconcerted, the young lady put the smile back where it came from and examined him with a suspicious eye.

"I know," Valentin went on, "that women get upset when people can't stick a name onto their face, and the one thing I desire at the present moment is not to upset you. So, Mademoiselle, may I ask you to do me a favor: help me to remember in what circumstances we met."

As the girl hasn't yet recovered her powers of speech, Valentin retains his and continues in these terms:

"I think I can guess. Aren't you from Bordeaux?"

"Me? from Bordeaux?" exclaims the girl, who has never known anyone to pull anything of this sort on her before, especially in the neighborhood of the Gare de l'Est.

"Yes. More precisely, from le Bouscat. I'll bet you're one of my wife's customers."

"Because you're married?"

Without noticing that she had called him *tu*, Valentin replied:

"Yes: we're even on our honeymoon."

"Ah! Right, then. Ought to have said so straight off."

And, turning her back on him, she directed her steps toward other suckers. But Valentin chased after her.

"Mademoiselle, Mademoiselle, you mustn't run away like that. I'm not frightening you, I hope."

But she still looked almost stern.

"You?!"

"You won't refuse to have a drink with me, will you?"

She hesitated, but as business wasn't so good as all that, she decided that it was reasonable to take the risk, and accepted. She led Valentin into a modest brasserie frequented by some of her colleagues. They were in the habit of taking a little break there before going back to walk the streets.

She accepted a peppermint drink and Valentin treated himself to a *vin blanc gommé*.

"Well then," she said, trying to make a bit of conversation and rise to the occasion, "so you're on your honeymoon?"

"Yes," replied Valentin, with great simplicity.

"And where's your wife at the moment?"

"In Bordeaux."

Two of her colleagues, drinking black coffee at the bar, hearing this dialogue, rambled over to Valentin's table and started listening unashamedly.

"You're putting me on," said the girl.

"Not at all," protested Valentin. "It's the honest truth. As witness the fact that I'm going to Bruges-la-Morte. Hm, mustn't miss my train."

"What time is it, your train?"

"Eleven twelve," replied Valentin, prudently.

"Well then, you've got lots of time to have a bit."

"I don't much feel like taking my shoes off," said Valentin.

The two colleagues intervened:

"If you've got time to waste," said one of them, "bully for you."

"Mado," said the other, "I never knew you were such a stupid cuntess. Can't you see he's taking you for a ride?"

Lamenting the misfortunes of the times and whatever you might not see next, they went and put their glasses back on the counter.

Palely furious, Mado plunked her two elbows down on the table and, leaning over toward Valentin, asked him:

"Are you coming up or are you not coming up?"

"I'm not coming up."

"Don't you like me?"

" 'Course I do."

"Don't you like my figure?"

" 'Course I do."

"Don't you think I can do it every bit as well as your virgin?"

"I don't know."

"Well then?"

"I'm not coming up," said Valentin. "I only wanted to have a drink with you. I thought that was so nice."

She turned to her two colleagues and called them to witness:

"No, but really, d'you hear this prick? Do you hear this prick?"

"We hear," said the other two with resignation. "We hear."

"I'm really very sorry," murmured Valentin.

Mado banged on the table:

"That's a good ten minutes I've been listening to your wise-cracks, and personally I don't reckon to work for nothing. Isn't that right?" she asked the other two.

"If we let them get away with it," said the one.

"That'd be the end," said the other.

"Perhaps these young ladies might have a drink with us?" suggested Valentin.

"We'll leave you," they said to Mado.

They threw some small change onto the counter and left.

"They're leaving you in the lurch," remarked Valentin, impartially.

"I can look after myself," said Mado.

"Don't have to. Don't have to. I'll compensate you."

"What for?"

"I'll give you what I would have given you if I'd come and taken my shoes off in your company."

"Are you nuts, or what?"

"It's only natural! What do I owe you?"

"Look, baby, d'you think I'm going to accept money I haven't earned, just like that? Who d'you take me for?"

She turned to the proprietor who was trying to read a newspaper upside down to pass the time:

"Did you hear him, Meussieu Grégoire? He's insulting me!"

"Take his cash and piss off, the both of you," declared Meussieu Grégoire laconically, without raising his eyes.

"You see," said Valentin to Mado. "How much is it, then?"

"Thirty francs," replied Mado, reluctantly.

Valentin, who had been directing his right hand toward his left wallet, stopped his hand in its tracks and let out a long whistle of surprise.

"Shit," he said, in all simplicity. "That's a lot."

"You aren't going to ask me to give you a reduction, I suppose," said Mado with a sneering laugh.

"No, but I can't help it, I think that's a lot. Almost as much as taxis."

"Oh! that'll do," said Mado. "Tightwads like you had just better not take taxis."

"I had a big suitcase; a very heavy one."

"What've you done with it?"

"I put it in the checkroom but when I came out I couldn't find the taxi."

"What the hell did that matter?"

"I hadn't paid the driver."

Meussieu Grégoire and Mado burst out laughing.

"Had you told him you were going to the checkroom," asked the boss, finally joining in the conversation.

"Naturally," said Valentin.

"Then you can be quite sure he's waiting for you there."

Valentin scratched his head.

"Now you're in the shit," said Mado, laughing.

He looked at her with a piteous expression.

"There's one thing you could do," exclaimed Meussieu Grégoire. "Mado could go and get it for you, your suitcase."

Mado gave him a quick glance.

"Of course," she agreed, becoming serious again.

Valentin seemed to be weighing the pros and cons, then he suddenly gets up and, before the other two have had time to react, he'd crossed the room, saying: "That's it, I'll go and get a taxi." At the door he turns round and, with a wink: "Hope I don't pick the same one!" Which makes Meussieu Grégoire and Mado laugh. He goes out, turns the first corner, gallops fearlessly until he gets to another, and finally comes to a big boulevard glittering with a thousand lights, in which he does indeed find a taxi stand. He gets into the first one without asking the driver's permission, and the latter hears himself asked to go to the Gare du Nord. The driver doesn't start driving, but turns round to his fare:

"I won't do it," says he.

Valentin is for a moment in two minds about whether he's going to ask him why not, but the other continues:

"I'm not going to let you waste your money. It's just up the street, the Gare du Nord. You can walk it in five minutes."

"But I've got a train in three minutes," objects Valentin, without much conviction.

"Not true. There's no train that leaves the Gare du Nord in three minutes. I know the departure times of all the trains for all the stations in Paris. What do you expect, after thirty years of taxi driving. Now my first jalopy was a Brasier, a real chauffeur-driven job. There weren't many of us in those days. It was quite something. And I did the Marne, yes I, Meussieu, under the orders of Joffre and Galliéni. You may be too young to have heard about that, the taxis of the Marne."

"No, no, I do know. The Marne, that was an interesting battle," said Valentin dreamily. "I do know. But what I'm especially interested in is Jena, the Battle of Jena."

"There's the bridge," said the driver mechanically, "and not only the Pont d'Iéna but the Place and the Avenue as well. And then there's the Passage, near the Porte Champerret."

Leaning over into a ray of light, Valentin consults his turnip.

"Would you like me to take you for a trip round those parts?" suggests the driver.

"I'd like it very much," replies Valentin, already won over, "but I don't know whether I've got time."

"I'll bet you're taking the eleven thirty-seven express for Boulogne?"

"You're very clever."

"Oh!" said the other modestly, "I guessed it right away. You were afraid of missing your train, isn't that true?"

"That is true."

"I tell you, I guessed it right away. Well then, would you like me to drive you to the Passage, after that we pass the Étoile, we go down the Avenue, we cross the Place, then the bridge, the Pont d'Iéna, we drive along the embankment, we cross the Seine again at the Place Saint-Michel, and we come back by the Boulevard Sébastopol. Does that suit you? Don't be afraid, you'll be at the Gare du Nord in time for your train."

Valentin, tempted, still hesitated.

"How much, about, is it going to set me back?" he asked courageously.

"You can see the whole lot for a louis."

"All that way for twenty francs?"

Valentin began to have doubts about the honesty of the other driver.

"Of course," replied this one. "And here, come and sit beside me, I'll explain the beauties of the capital to you, because I've also guessed that you don't come from these parts. Correct?"

"Correct."

Obeying the order he had been given, Valentin went and sat in the place indicated.

VII

ENCHANTED WITH his trip, Valentin warmly shook the driver's hand. But brought back on the dot for the eleven-thirty train, he went and sojourned in the double-you-see until five minutes before the departure of his. He bought his ticket in haste, and caught his train just in time, and this without having met anyone.

At Bruges he had a few little difficulties because of his lack of baggage. He had to pay for his room every night, couldn't change his clothes and went to the barber every other day. Twelve days passed thus.

Back in Paris, he decided to abandon his suitcase, although he regretted it, it had been through the campaign against the Merina Hain-Tenys with him. He would say that someone had swiped it. It happens to everyone, to have things stolen. Doesn't mean you're more of a jerk than the next fellow. And then, like that he had his hands free, which is extremely pleasant when you want to do a lot of walking. And in fact he did do a lot of walking and only just missed the Gare d'Austerlitz, since three hours after his departure from the Gare du Nord he was walking up the rue de Charenton. This long and varied thoroughfare interested him extremely. The plaque on the wall of No. 306 seemed to him one of the great curiosities of Paris: "It is expressly prohibited to build beyond the present boundaries and limits, etc. 1726." One more stupid prohibition. Numerous houses beyond it were sufficient proof. He admired from a distance a majestic cupola which he attributed to the Sacré-Coeur although it actually belonged to the Saint-Esprit, and soon afterward saw, outlined against the horizon to his right, a magnificent freight depot.

As he was walking very slowly, so as not to miss anything of the landscape, he was passed by a funeral: an extremely modest procession, with neither priest nor circumstance; a hearse of great purity of line towed by an ancient old nag and followed by less than ten people. They say that it's always very interesting to attach yourself to unknown people's funeral processions; they can very often occasion strange encounters. Valentin knew that that was only one of the old platitudes that people trot out without really believing them but which, if you put them into practice, sometimes turn out to be true, like: "great oaks from little acorns grow," but knowing that he was somewhat out of his depth he decided to put to the test the credence people might place in the proverb: "he who follows others to earth, ends up on the bandwagon." Attaching himself to the rear of the procession, then, he continued his walk. He had still not spoken to anyone when they arrived at the Réuilly cemetery. A fellow in front, with great big ears, vaguely reminded him of someone or something, but he was just about to abandon his suspicions, thinking that the dictum was just as false as all the others when one of the people at the head of the cortège turned round (to see what?) and he thought he recognized Julia.

And it was Julia. It was indeed Julia. When the coffin (containing whom? containing what?) had been lowered into the grave and the family comprising four people had marshaled themselves into a horizontal line to receive the condolences of the five other members of the cortège, and when said condolences having been offered, said persons had departed, a sixth stepped forward, warmly shook Bretaga's hand, then, with emotion, that of Chantal, and finally he was just about to put even more feeling into the hand-sheikh he was reserving for Julia, when she recognized him.

"Well for crying out loud!" she exclaimed. "Valentin!"

She flung her arms round his neck.

"Hello, my beloved! Hello, my angel!"

And, turning to the other two:

"What a joke, eh?"

"Well I don't know," said Paul.

"Talk about a surprise," Chantal opined.

It made them all laugh, especially Julia.

"But what the hell were you doing there?" asked Paul.

"Just going for a walk," replied Valentin.

"What a laugh he is," said Chantal.

"By the way," exclaimed Valentin, "I've got something for you."

He searched his pocket and brought out a crumpled post card depicting the Gare de l'Est. Having verified the address, he handed it to the Brutagas.

"This is for you," he said.

Then he pulled out a second one, which he put back in his pocket having observed that it was intended for Sergeant Bourrelier. He hoped that with a bit of luck he would avoid the one that he'd meant to send to Didine. But that was precisely the one he picked on. Then he once again brought out the one for Sergeant Bourrelier.

"There isn't one for me, then?" asked Julia, cackling.

"Hold on," said Valentin.

"That was nice of you, to think of us," said the Brebugas in chorus, having deciphered the message on the reverse side, the one reserved for correspondence.

"It's only natural," retorted Valentin, lightly.

Finally he found the card for Julia.

"My pet! aren't you sweet!" she howled.

Having read the text, she adds, laughing:

"Well, you didn't exactly strain yourself."

Valentin laughed with her, and the other two with them.

"And what about Bruges?" asked Julia. "You did go to Bruges?"

"As you see," replied Valentin.

"Was it nice?"

"There's something to be said on both sides."

"Well but, are you satisfied?"

"Oh ye-ess."

She kissed him again, and then stepped back.

"No but really," she remarked, "you stink."

"Who, me?"

"Yes, you. Not the pope."

Valentin had begun to frown, but this soon turned into a broad smile and an air of extreme satisfaction.

"I know why," he said triumphantly. "I haven't changed my clothes for a fortnight."

"Isn't he a laugh," said Chantal.

"You took plenty of shirts with you, though," observed Julia.

"I lost my suitcase," said Valentin. "That's to say, I didn't exactly lose it. But it's about the same."

"Where is it?"

"In the checkroom at the Gare du Nord."

"But you haven't lost the ticket?" asked Paul.

"No."

"Then all you have to do is go and get it."

"So it is," said Valentin.

They were all silent for a moment.

"Isn't he a laugh," said Chantal.

A gravedigger came up and asked them if they were going to stay there much longer. Not that they, the family, were in their way, but it was time for them, the gravediggers, to go to lunch, and they, the gravediggers, would only finish filling it, the hole, in, after they had had it, their lunch.

"Take your time, my good men," said Paul. "It's quite all right as it is: there's enough to stop him getting out."

Everyone laughed politely at this witticism.

"Let's get out of here then, eh?" said Julia.

"You must all come and have lunch at our place," declared Chantal. "Are you coming too?"

The person she thus addressed uttered a grunt which was taken to be a reply in the affirmative.

"We'll try and find a cab," said Jules, leading the way.

Valentin smiled. Taxis, he was a connoisseur of taxis, now.

"You think we won't find one?" asked Paul, with the susceptibility of a brother-in-law.

"I don't know," replied Valentin, immediately becoming serious again.

They walked ahead, the two of them, escorted by the three women. Valentin thought he ought to make himself pleasant so he starts a conversation.

"Do you know the person we've just interred?" he asks gravely.

"No," replies Paul. "I'd never seen him."

"Just like me."

"I don't doubt it," retorts Paul, with a little neighing sound.

"Do you often follow funerals, just like that?"

"It's sort of cyclic. Haven't you noticed? Sometimes you don't go to a burial for two or three years, at other times there's one every week, or almost."

"Today, was it a funeral or a burial?"

Paul gives Valentin a dubious look out of the corner of his eye.

"Neither the one nor the other: just shoveling a lousy carcass into the ground."

Now it's Valentin's turn to look at Paul out of the corner of his eye, amazed at the vigor of his language.

"Wow," he ejaculates, in an admiring exhalation.

"It's just what I said."

And Bratragra lowers his eyes modestly.

Valentin, having got his breath back, continues in an inquisitive, and, at least in theory, logical, fashion:

"But, but, but! you did—you *did* know the person? You told me just now that you didn't know who it was."

"There's knowing and knowing," grunted Paul, "just as there's funerals and burials."

"Snot clear," said Valentin, irritated.

Paul stops suddenly and grabs his brother-in-law by the lapel of his jacket, which obliged Valentin to stop likewise.

"You," said Brébaga, "don't really suppose, do you, that I was following, that we were following, a funeral without knowing who was in between the four planks?"

"The six," objected Valentin.

With three gestures he explained what he meant, thus freeing himself from the clutches of his brother-in-law, who didn't insist.

"You're right," said Paul. "Between the six planks."

"That's right, isn't it?"

And Valentin made himself pleasant.

The ladies caught up with them and Paul suggested that

they should make for the gate and try and grab a cab. Everyone agreed, and once again the two men walked ahead, followed at a distance by the women who went on chewing the fat with some animation.

Abandoning the theme of the identity of the deceased person, Valentin switched the conversation on to a new track by inquiring about the civil status of the lady who was flanked by Chantal and Julia. Mechanically, Paul glanced behind him and replied:

"It's the pope."

Valentin likewise glanced behind him and said resolutely, albeit modestly:

"You'll never get me to believe that."

Paul started sniggering and replied, very simply:

"It's true, though."

Suddenly, he simultaneously stopped laughing and walking, and struck himself on the bean. Valentin stepped back a couple of paces to prevent the other fellow buttonholing him once again, that was something he couldn't abide.

"It's true, though!" he exclaimed. "Good God!"

He seemed illuminated by his discovery, but undecided: was he going to transform it into uncontrollable laughter, or into oratorical procedures?

"What an idiot I am!" said he, choosing the second course.

"You don't have to tell us," said Chantal, who had come up with the other two women.

"And what about that taxi?" asked Julia. "Do *I* have to find it?"

"Mesdames, have you not noticed something," he asked with a wily look.

"We don't give a damn what you've noticed," said Chantal.

"I'm as hungry as a fighting cock," said Julia.

"Some of us are going to be hungry for ordinary cocks," concludes the third woman, lugubriously.

Valentin examines her with interest. She wears her years well-encapsulated in blubber, and her mourning clothes with numerous blobs of similar substances. She is patently avoiding casting her eyes on human beings, or at least on those here present. She seems to prefer the contemplation of the objects littering the ground, or else, abruptly, she follows exactly the flight of a passing bird, but without moving her head, and it is a noble head.

As her intervention has caused a silence, she takes advantage of it to yawn noisily.

"Well?" she asks, turning her back on them.

Then she faces them again and yawns a second time in sonorous fashion.

"We might perhaps have a drink," Paul suggested, in a flabby voice.

They agreed, even though this didn't get them any farther, and as they were in Paris there was no shortage of bistros and it was only the choice that was difficult.

It was still warm enough for them to relish the charms of the terrace, where they sit down in a circle.

"Well, my little man," said Julia, grabbing hold of Valentin's cheek between her thumb and index finger, "are you still satisfied?"

"I am," replied Valentin, with a broad smile.

Meanwhile a waiter appears. He is patient and distant. He is thinking of things other than those which surround him. He awaits the order with neither haste nor repugnance. Paul addresses him haughtily:

"Tell me, eh, don't they know what a taxi is in these parts?"

"That any of your business?" replied the waiter calmly.

"Indeed it is. We intended to take one."

"Ought to have said so."

Suddenly he notices their mourning.

"Someone in the family?" he asks solicitously.

"Her boyfriend," replies Chantal, pointing to the old woman with her thumb.

"You'd never believe it," says Julia, "but at the age of sixty-seven she went and set up house with a creep. At sixty-seven! What d'you think of that, eh?"

"Love's a child that's gypsy-born," replies the waiter sententiously.

"You don't think it's ridiculous?"

Julia is highly amazed by this indulgence. The waiter smiles:

"In love, Mademoiselle, nothing is ridiculous."

"D'you hear that?" she says to her sister, pinching her arm. "He called me 'Mademoiselle'!"

She wags a finger at the waiter:

"You're a brigand," she simpers. "A brigand!"

"What a dope," says Paul.

The old woman, who seemed to be diligently studying the circular structure of the waiter's tray, the old woman slowly begins to look at someone, and this someone is Paul. Paul pales, and pretends to be watching the street, you never know, a taxi might go by.

"Well," says the waiter, in conclusion, "what's done is done. So like that," he adds, addressing his remarks in familiar fashion to the old bag, "now Madame is a widow twice over."

"She can't be a widow," says Chantal scornfully, "she wasn't married."

"And what about the other time, doesn't that make me a widow?" retorts the old woman threateningly.

"Oh yes, oh yes," Chantal hastens to agree.

But something is bothering Julia. She interpolates the waiter.

"Hey, you, why did you say: 'Now Madame is a widow twice over.' How did you know?"

"He didn't know," says Chantal, "seeing that she's only been a widow once."

"Maybe we might order," says Paul, irritated; he's recovered from his emotion. "It's getting late. The lunch'll be spoilt."

"You bug us," says Julia.

"I'd certainly like to eat, one of these days," says the old girl.

Paul triumphs. He attracts attention by clicking his fingers like a schoolboy:

"Bring us five vermouths, waiter—five Turin-Cassis—and make it snappy!"

But Julia isn't going to let the waiter go like that: she has been tossing and re-tossing his remarks in the frying pan of her critical intelligence. Finally the bubble bursts:

"You're a bloody fucking son of a bitch of a whore," she tells him. "Calling me Mademoiselle, when I'm with my husband!"

Valentin rises from his chair a fraction, to show that he is the person in question.

"You probably think he's my gigolo," she continues, "and that we didn't get ourselves legitimized by Msieu the Mayor. It's disgusting to be insulted like that. I won't stay here five minutes more," she concludes, without budging.

"Things are hotting up," remarks Paul under his breath.

Valentin stands up and, as if everyone were following him, leaves.

He's gone.

VIII

When Ganière arrived to open the store, she found outside it a guy sitting on an overnight case bound with aluminum strips. The individual in question, even though he hadn't shaved, was methodically cleaning his nails with a toothpick. Ganière recognized her boss's husband. Much affected, she greeted him.

"I was just passing," said he calmly, "only unfortunately I didn't have the keys. Am I disturbing you?"

"Not at all," stammered Ganière, terrorized.

She tried to put a key in a lock, but her hand was trembling. Valentin came to her aid.

"You know, Msieu," said Ganière, "Madame isn't here. She's away."

"And where's 'away'?"

"She's gone to the funeral of the meussieu who was living in sin with her mother in Paris," replied Ganière at top speed.

"Good, good," said Valentin absently. "Carry on with your work, don't bother about me. I'll take my suitcase up, have a shave and come down again."

"You're going to do that?" asked Ganière, frightened to death.

"No doubt," replied Valentin, looking at her vaguely. "And then," he added, for his own benefit, "I'm going to change my clothes."

He smiled at her, and winked.

"I stink," he explained.

He did as he had said and, half an hour later, came down again from the apartment on the first floor. He found Ganière in the middle of the store; she seemed not to have moved in the meantime.

"How's business? All right?" he asked her, sitting down on a chair.

She jumped. Her eyes starting out of her head, she didn't answer.

"Madame isn't here," she started to say again, distraught.

"I'll wait for her."

He looked around him.

"It's nice, here," he remarked, trying to make himself pleasant to this girl. "I never really noticed, before. I was too busy," he added, with a smile. "In any case, though, I've got to get used to it."

The girl was still gaping. Valentin went on:

"It'll make less work for you, if I'm here as well. I'll give you a hand. I'll start by helping with the little things."

He stood up, which resulted in Ganière's rapid retreat toward the street door. Not appearing to be surprised, he went over to some shelves on which there were piles of buttons of every conceivable variety. A specimen was sewn on to each little box; and several, if they came in different sizes.

"There's some pretty ones," said Valentin, inspecting them attentively. "Those, for example."

He was pointing to some pink glass ones with silvery streaks. Not having had any answer, he turned round and observed that Ganière had taken off. Without bothering his head, he pursued his examination, even venturing to open various drawers to see what was in them. Then he became lost in the amazement that the cash register engendered in him.

A customer finally came in. She looked around her anxiously, wondering whether she was going to address herself to this meussieu. As this meussieu was content to look at her with curiosity, but with mute curiosity, the good woman decides to make the first move and expresses herself in these terms:

"Isn't Mademoiselle Segovia here?"

"Mademoiselle Segovia is no more."

"What?" exclaims the lady, bringing both her hands up to her heart.

"Don't worry, Madame, don't worry. I simply meant that Mademoiselle Segovia had become Madame Brû."

"Pff, that's all the same to me. And anyway, everyone knows that, young man. You think you're telling me something I don't know? But for all Mademoiselle Segovia's customers, Mademoiselle Segovia will always remain Mademoiselle Segovia."

"You're what they call a faithful customer."

"Very nicely put. And do you know why, young man?"

"No, but I soon will."

Flustered, the lady asked:

"How will you?"

"I shall listen to you."

Full of suspicion, she reflected for a few moments, but, as she didn't know what to reflect on, she lost the thread of her argument.

"What was I saying?" she asked.

"You weren't saying anything," replied Valentin.

The lady fell silent, full of misgivings.

"And how's your husband?" asked Valentin.

"Not at all well," replied the lady. "He's soaking it up."

"Another alcoholic," sighed Valentin.

"So you guessed?"

Valentin lowered his eyes modestly.

The good lady couldn't get over it.

"Here," said Valentin, standing up, "would you like to see these buttons?"

He brought out the box of the pink glass ones with the silvery streak, and opened it.

"Pretty, aren't they?"

He held them up and made them sparkle in a ray of the pale October sun.

Then he shut the box and put it back in its place.

"I don't want to sell them," he declared. "I really want to keep them for my collection. I'm going to collect buttons. In this one," he said, designating the shelves around the shop with a sweeping gesture, "there aren't any, for example, of the 13th Colonial Regiment, a military unit to which I had the honor to belong."

"My little boy collects streetcar tickets," said the lady.

"That's interesting, too," Valentin conceded.

He searched his pocket and pulled out a little paper pellet which he carefully smoothed out.

"Here, what a bit of luck. This one's from Bruges. They're very rare. A fine item for your kid's collection."

"Oh! but I wouldn't like to."

"Oh but do, do."

"It's really too kind of you."

She looked at the bit of paper with respect:

"Bruges," she murmured. "And have you used it?"

"Yes, Madame."

"You've traveled, Meussieu."

"So little, Madame, so little."

"Even so. The farthest I've ever been to is Royan."

"You see."

"What I'd really like is Mont Saint-Michel."

"Me too, but most of all Jena."

"Don't know it."

"It's a battlefield."

"Oh! thanks a lot! One day someone offered me a trip to go and look at the trenches of the nineteen-fourteen-to-eighteen war, and well, even though I haven't traveled a lot, I replied: wars, we don't ever want any more, and I never went."

"That's what they call having the courage of your convictions."

"Quite so."

A little pause. She goes on:

"You know, you sure do talk nicely."

She runs her eyes over him with a captivated-captivating look.

"My treasure!" comes a howl. "My angel, my little sugar plum!"

Julia flings her arms round Valentin's neck and covers his face with sonorous kisses. Behind her an elderly lady has come in, covered in violet-, indigo-, blue-, green-, yellow-, orange-, and red-colored finery. This person immediately sits down at the cash desk, leans her elbows on it and looks up at the ceiling, where she studies the comings and goings of the last flies of the season.

Having meted out to Valentin his osculatory ration, Julia turns to the customer:

"But it's Madame Panigère! Good morning, Madame Panigère! And how's your love life? Is Meussieu Panigère still nice and stiff? Oh! Madame Panigère, you've got rings round your eyes this morning. You've had another hell of a night. Don't deny it, don't deny it. I'm sure Meussieu Panigère has nothing to complain of in you. I'll bet you're always the one that asks for more. Don't deny it, don't deny it. And my little husband, what d'you think of him? Good-looking boy, eh? Ah ha ha, Madame Panigère, don't look at him with sheep's eyes like that or I'll throw you out. My little husband, he's mine. Hands off! Got it? Heh heh, could Meussieu Panigère be slipping? Madame Panigère, I'm beginning to believe you're looking for a boyfriend. Don't deny it, don't deny it. Personally, you understand, I wouldn't give a shit if you made Meussieu Panigère wear horns, but not me, not me. And anyway, he loves me like mad, like anything, like anything, like anything, my Valentin does. Correct?"

"Of course," said Valentin.

"Look here, Madame Panigère, I can prove it. After we'd buried a creep whose name I don't even want to mention, that was why I was away, I had to go to Paris for the ceremony."

"And you went all the way to Paris just to bury a creep, to use your own expression?" asked Madame Panigère in admiring tones.

"Precisely. Family solidarity. Well, to cut a long story short, this was yesterday morning. In the first place, something comic: when we got to the cemetery we noticed that there was someone following the procession that we hadn't noticed was following it, and guess who that someone was? My Valentin."

"Well I never," said Madame Panigère who, being a bit thick, didn't really appreciate the comic side of this event.

"Eh? A bit out of the ordinary?"

"Well yes, you could say that," conceded Madame Panigère.

"After that, we all go for a drink, only natural, hm? We sit down on a café terrace, not bothering anyone, and next thing you know the waiter starts insulting me. My blood boils and I say: 'I'm not going to stay a moment longer in a rotten dump like this, let's fuck off.' Well, the only one who actually fucked off was my Valentin. Don't you think that was nice?"

"Indeed it was," says Madame Panigère.

"All the more so seeing that he was the only one who left."

"He had the courage of his convictions," says Madame Panigère.

"Oh! oh! oh!" exclaims Madame Brû. "Well, what do you know, Madame Panigère, so my Valentin has already been giving you a line! I recognize one of those wisecraps he comes out with from time to time. Watch out! Madame Panigère. Watch out! Or I'll show my claws. Actually, what was it you wanted, Madame Panigère?"

"I was looking for some buttons for my pastel-colored blouse, Mademoiselle Segovia."

"I've just gotten some very pretty ones in. A novelty from Paris. Made of glass. With a silvery streak. I'll show you."

She went to find them. Madame Panigère examines them in silence, very attentively.

"They're pretty," she finally says, "but I thought you didn't want to sell them."

"Me? Not sell?"

Such a thought covered her with shame.

"Meussieu told me so," declared Madame Panigère, indicating Valentin with her head, but taking good care not to look at him.

"Him? but he doesn't know anything about it."

"He even wants to keep them all."

Madame Panigère adds, with a touch of scorn:

"To make a collection of them."

"If you have no objection," says Valentin.

"If I have no objection! *And how* I have an objection! Who's ever seen a storekeeper refuse to sell something he's got in his store?"

"You think so?" asked Valentin, not entirely convinced.

"Do I think so! And how I think so! And then, you aren't going to start collecting buttons! Or even collecting anything whatsoever."

"It was an idea I wasn't so specially sold on," said Valentin.

"You see?" said Julie to Madame Panigère. "You see how sweet he is, and not contrary. He's a real little husband. And how many do you want?"

"The whole box," replied Valentin.

"That'll be rather a lot for one blouse," remarked Julia, going over to the cash desk.

"Madame is taking some for her apple-green blouse too," said Valentin.

"Hm, I didn't know you had one," said Julia, absorbed in wrapping up the buttons.

Suddenly she jumped.

"And Ganière? Where's Ganière? Where is that little slut? That'll be eighteen francs, Madame Panigère, yes but after all, a whole box is a luxury that everyone can't treat themselves to. But you'll see, you'll be very pleased with them and they're guaranteed—a genuine Paris novelty. There we are, Madame Panigère. No, I thank you. Good-by, Madame Panigère. And don't tire your husband out, Madame Panigère. Don't deny it, don't deny it. Yes, where's that slut Ganière? She's been getting herself tumbled again, the little hooker. Tell all, what happened to you? You came back by the first train? Huh, I knew you would! So you arrived at eleven o'clock. You slept in the station? You hadn't any money left to get yourself a room? And your suitcase? Did you get it back? Good, good. Well, so there we are, then."

She sat down on a chair, legs apart, smiling with satisfaction. The old lady, after having activated the cash harvester with startling self-assurance, resumed her study of the maneuvers of the flies on the ceiling. Valentin was absentmindedly playing about with a wooden ruler he'd found on one of the counters.

"What are you thinking about?" asked the old lady.

66

"There's a couple of centimeters missing," Valentin immediately answered.

Julia cast an incredulous glance in his direction.

"Nanette," she said, "don't be too impressed. I told him so myself. It's true, though," she added, stretching, without getting up out of her chair, "you don't know each other."

With a weary gesture she extended her left arm:

"My husband, Valentin Brû, ex-private soldier."

Then her right arm:

"My mother, Nanette. Yesterday's widow."

Yawning, she added:

"And tomorrow's."

Then, changing the subject:

"I'm sleepy. I can never manage to sleep in a train. Aren't *you* sleepy?"

"No," replied Nanette bluntly.

"Well, *I*'m going to change my shoes and then I'm going to have a nap until lunchtime. If any customers come, toss 'em out. As for Ganière, when she comes back, tell her to wait for me, I've got a word or two to say to her."

Having thus distributed her orders, she went upstairs to lie down.

Nanette and Valentin resumed their several occupations in silence: the former, the flies; the latter, the centimeters. From time to time he looked covertly at the old girl, his rapid glance observing the dress heavily corroded with sweat under the armpits, a whole bazaar hanging down over her chest, the bulky, sparkling rings on every finger.

A lady came in. Surprised not to see the proprietress, her glance oscillated between the woman at the cash desk and the fellow holding a rule in his hand. Finally she opted for the fellow, a young man who looked extremely amiable.

"I," says she to him, "would like seventy-five centimeters of zip fastener."

"Madame and I," replied Valentin amiably, "are not qualified to serve you. The directrix of this establishment has no intention of indulging in any commercial activity whatsoever this morning."

"What? What? Where's Mzelle Segovia?"

"She's asleep."

"That's a good one."

"My word of honor. Perhaps you are not acquainted with her mother? She is the lady seated at the cash desk. As for me, I am her husband."

"What? Mzelle Segovia has got married?"

"I am the living proof of that. But do please sit down."

"Don't mind if I do, that's taken the ground from under my feet. When she always used to say that all men were bastards, pimps, and drunks."

"She still thinks so," said Valentin gravely. "Doesn't she, Nanette?"

IX

NANETTE LOOKED great with her burial chinstrap. They wrapped her up carefully and took her to the Reuilly cemetery.

They shook hands with the loyal tradespeople, with divers anonymous personages and, when these had dispersed, with the nonmembers of the family.

"To think that it's less than six months," sighed Paul.

"The undertakers must be thinking that they only see us and the dicky-birds," said Valentin.

So as not to have to chase after a taxi, they'd hired a car.

"I little thought, last time I was here, that I'd be back so soon," said Paul gravely.

"You remember what you said to me that day?" said Valentin. "These things always go in series."

"Doesn't surprise anyone that you said such a bloody stupid thing," said Julie, and she added:

"You didn't bring her luck."

Paul bridled:

"That's going a bit far. Anyone might think I killed her."

"Why not?" said Julie, with sensational insincerity. "You never know, do you?"

"You're the one that people should be making insinuations about. Who had an interest in her popping off? Who was looking after her at the last?"

"Us," said Valentin, replying impartially to both questions.

"You see," said Julie to Paul, "you agree that we were looking after her. If we were looking after her, that means that we didn't kill her."

"Apart from that," said Chantal, "you've certainly made us look like a couple of half-witted cunts."

"Kindly express yourself with less vulgarity," said Julia.

"Have to say what is," retorted Chantal. "You've collared practically the whole of the inheritance. In the first place the store in the rue Brèche-aux-Loups. And next, all you extracted from her since then."

"That's mere supposition," said Julia calmly.

"We'll see about that with the lawyer," said Paul calmly.

"Go ahead and see the lawyer," said Julia calmly.

"There may be a will that restores justice," said Paul fervently.

"You rely on that, my little man," said Julia calmly.

They get out of the car, Valentin pays the driver, they'd discussed the price beforehand, the funeral lunch is at the Brûs', seeing that last time it was at the Bratugras'. Julia goes into her bedroom to change her shoes, Valentin notices that there isn't any more aperitif and hurries off to get some.

"Even so," says Chantal under her breath, "they've certainly ripped us off in a big way."

"And how," agrees Paul bitterly.

"Especially him," says Chantal.

"Yes, there's no denying it, he took the old girl in like I'd never have been able to."

"Oh! you."

"Did you notice? In no more than six months of buttering her up he got the store and the cash out of her."

"He knew how to go about it."

"And what's more, the old girl goes and croaks just when he doesn't need her any more."

"D'you think he put a little something in her nightcap?"

"Makes you wonder."

"Ought to have a post-mortem."

"That'd cost money."

"You say all this and that and then you climb down. Do you think he killed her or don't you?"

"I don't."

"You see?"

"What do I see?"

"That you're talking out of the back of your head. Valentin wouldn't hurt a fly."

"Oh! you!—you've got a thing about him."

"That's news to me."

"I mean, he fools you like he fooled Nanette. Actually, you admire him for having taken us in. And yet he got away with it under your very nose, your mother's inheritance. All you're going to get out of it is the chicken you'll be eating any minute now. What's more it'll be tough, because Julia's grub is always terrible."

"Quite true," said Valentin, putting a bottle down on the table. "She doesn't keep her maids long enough. They only have to ask me: Would Meussieu rather have pork or veal? and she throws them out. She's so jealous," he concludes, with amused indulgence. "Hell, we haven't got a corkscrew. I'll go and get one from the kitchen. Have you seen the new one?"

He leaned over toward them and murmured:

"She's a monster."

Paul went and looked at the bottle.

"They do themselves proud," he said scornfully. "Sandeman port. They're quite shameless. It's Nanette's cash they've bought it with, their port! Our cash! Ah! bloody fucking assholes, why on earth didn't we prevent that marriage! At least *I* tried. But you! You did everything possible to bring it about! Even going so far as to sleep with Captain Bordeille! The others, there was always a more or less valid reason. But Captain Bordeille! Just one thing leading to another, to get an inheritance snatched away from under your very nose. How stupid can you get?"

"I wonder why Julia had to tell you."

"All I can do now is work even harder than ever," declaimed Paul. "So that our daughter can have a dowry."

"Talk about dead cats," said Chantal, smoothing her stockings at the memory of Captain Bordeille.

Paul activated his shoulders in all directions. Deeply moved by the abnegation of which he had just given evidence, he was fondling, with fluttering fingers, the flagon of Sandeman port.

"What's he up to?" he grumbled.

"He's fucking the monster," replied Chantal.

"That's all you ever think of," observed Paul bitterly. "Hm," he exclaimed, "I've got an idea."

Chantal didn't say: that'd be the day, she'd given up. Whereas Julia, she couldn't stop herself saying it. But she wasn't there to do so; she was changing her shoes. It was thus in silence that Bataga brought out of his pocket a Swiss knife with thirty-seven blades plus a corkscrew. He carefully removed the capsule of lead around the cork.

"Make yourself at home," said Valentin, coming back with the desired object. "One corkscrew is as good as another corkscrew, it's only the neck of the bottle that counts. Right?"

He sat down comfortably and watched his brother-in-law getting red in the face trying to master the bottle.

"They're well corked, eh, those?" he said solicitously.

He turned to Chantal:

"He's going to give himself a hernia."

"Don't worry," said Chantal. "He'll never do himself an injury opening a bottle."

"My goodness, Chantal, what a gorgeous bag you've got. The very latest fashion."

"How d'you know it's the latest fashion?" said Chantal, laughing.

"I saw it in *Marie-Claire*."

"What bag?" asked Paul, interrupting his extraction.

He glanced at it. A new one. He hadn't noticed. He goes back to his work.

Chantal leans over toward Valentin, showing her legs up to mid-thigh. She murmurs to him:

"You weren't very fair to us."

"Too true," says Valentin lightly.

"I wonder whether we couldn't take you to court."

"Hell."

"For misappropriation of an inheritance."

"That'd be amusing," says Valentin. "I'd never imagined myself in a court of law."

"In the dock," Paul resumed, at the same time as the port was saying: pp'ahh.

"Of course it would be even more amusing to be the judge," Valentin acknowledged. "All the same, now I'm a licenced tradesman I could be on a jury one day: I saw that in the paper."

"While you're waiting, we could sue you," said Chantal.

"Would I have to have a lawyer to defend me?" asked Valentin anxiously. "I'd rather do it myself."

"You haven't been doing too badly up to now," said Chantal, with some malice.

"Anyone want some?" asked Paul, who had already drunk a whole glass of Sandeman just to taste it, and had poured himself out a second one.

We'll empty their bottle for them, he kept telling himself furiously. This vengeance pleased him all the more in that he had no difficulty in effecting it.

"Of course we want some," said Chantal.

He handed them a couple of full glasses, while emptying his own to leave room for the contents of a third.

Chantal and Valentin touched glasses. Valentin smiled at Chantal:

"You won't make trouble for me, will you? In any case, you know, I just did the best I could, in all honesty. Nanette had taken a fancy to me, when she made her store over to me."

"Dirt cheap," said Paul.

"Not dirt cheap, just cheap. Yes, well, I didn't want to hurt her feelings. She was already so sad because of the death of her old man. And anyway, as you know, she didn't survive him six months. Don't you think that was fine?"

"Fine feelings went out with her generation," said Chantal.

"I'm not expecting you to wilt on my grave," said Paul, who

was beginning to think that life seen through port-rose-colored spectacles was a great deal more cordial than life seen through Pernod-green ditto, which always comprises a certain admixture of aggressivity.

"What about you?" Chantal asked Valentin.

"I don't think I shall die on Paul's grave, either."

This witticism made them crylaugh with real tears.

"But you might on Julia's?" asked Chantal.

Valentin thought this over.

"While we're on the subject," he said, "she, Julia, surely she . . ."

"Shells sea-sells," said Paul, incidentally.

". . . 's told you that in our marriage contract, hers and mine, the residue goes to the surviving partner. Just in case you might still have any vague hopes."

"Let's not talk any more about that," said Paul good-naturedly. "The whole thing's dead and buried. In a manner of speaking," he added, with a knowing look.

He helped himself to his fifth glass of port, observing with pleasure that the bottle would be finished before lunch.

"Is there any left?" asked Julie, coming in.

She knocked back the glass Paul handed her and sat down in an armchair, breathing hard.

"What were you chatting about?" she asked, without much conviction.

"About Mamma, of course," said Chantal.

"Pore Mamma," said Julia listlessly. "Pore Nanette," she added, with a bit more warmth. "Pore Mamma," she repeated, with unflagging sadness. "Pore Nanette. Pore Mamma."

She ended up sobbing, and stammering: "Mamma, Mamma."

"There, there," said Chantal, sitting down on the arm of the chair and putting her arm round her.

"That won't bring her back," said Paul optimistically.

"You never know," said Valentin. "If it's never worked, could well be because no one's ever cried long enough."

"You be quiet, you and your funny jokes," said Chantal. "You're going to put idiotic ideas into this poor girl's head."

"Come and get it," said the monster, appearing in the doorway.

"I was beginning to feel a bit empty," said Paul.

"Come on," said Chantal to her sister, "it'll give you something else to think about."

Julia got up, sniffing.

"Let's finish the bottle," Paul suggested.

He distributed the port around and about and, triumphantly, finished the bottle himself. He'd got his own back on these Brûs, with their aperitif bought out of his share of the inheritance.

"Our very good health!" he exclaimed.

They touched glasses and, once the Sandeman had reinvigorated Julie, they went into the dining room which, though diminutive, was furnished in pure nineteen-o-five style. The moment he set foot in the room Valentin perceived an agglomeration that dismayed him. It was oysters.

Thanks to a crafty policy of silence, he had thus far managed things so that, even though they had just traversed the winter months, it would never occur to Julia to include these ostreicultivated animals on the menu. But the monster, left to her own devices for once, had made no mistake: she had chosen, by instinct, what he most abominated.

He had scarcely outlined a plan of action before the other three had already gulped down half a dozen oysters apiece.

"Aren't you having any?" asks Julia. "They're fabulous."

"Not hungry."

"Don't have to be hungry to eat oysters."

"Isn't it a bit late in the season?"

"We're still in April."

"You can't get any good shellfish round these parts."

"They come from the Bastille."

"I'm keeping myself for the chicken."

"Risn't a chicken. There's *boeuf miroton*."

"Great," said Paul, gulping down the mollusks.

He was in perfect spirits. His thoughts were happily drifting over an ocean of disinterested ideas.

"Tell me, Valentin, are there any rhododendrons in Madagascar?"

"Oh, go stuff your rhododendrons," said Julia. "But tell *me*, Valentin—could it be that by any chance you don't like oysters?"

"Not all that much," replied Valentin pusillanimously.

"You mean you hate them."

"I don't eat them."

"And why not?"

"Because they're alive."

The other three stopped in their tracks, holding in the air their tridents transfixing a flabby, goblike mollusk.

"What's that you say?" asked Julia in a sodden voice.

"I say that they're alive. Personally, I don't eat living creatures."

"You aren't really going to tell me that these things are alive?"

"They're only just alive," said Paul.

"They're just as alive as you and me," said Valentin.

"Funny comparisons you make," said Julia.

"It's true, though," said Valentin. "An oyster, it's a living creature. Just as much as I am. Zno difference. Zonly one difference: between the living and the dead."

"You aren't very tactful," said Chantal.

"What I wonder," said Paul opportunely to Valentin, "is why you and Chantal don't call each other *tu*."

"You aren't going to tell me this is alive," said Julia, examining her animal attentively. "It hasn't got any eyes."

"Nor have sea urchins," retorted Valentin.

"They aren't animals," rejoined Julia, "they're fruit. Every self-respecting oyster seller calls them *fruits de mer*."

She swallowed her oyster.

"In any case," she added, laughing, "they're beasties that don't put up much of a fight. They go down as easy as winking."

Chantal and Jules swallowed theirs, though with less conviction.

"Look," said Valentin, leaning over toward Chantal who was at that moment squeezing a lemon onto the flesh of one of the lamellibranchia lying in her plate, "you see, when the acid falls on it, it shrinks."

Chantal looked at the phenomenon, terrified.

"It's true, though," she murmured.

"I won't argue the point with Valentin," said Paul, keeping his distance from his prospective victim, "he's perfectly right: they *are* animals, and even living animals."

He put down his trident and once again came back to the problem of the existence of the rhododendron in Madagascar. What did Valentin think?

"I don't think I ever saw any there," replied the latter.

"What did you see there? In the plant line?"

"A lot of them are exotic," said Valentin.

"You don't often talk about Madagascar," remarked Chantal, still calling him *vous*.

"Oh, call him *tu*," said Paul, "he's your brother-in-law. A brother-in-law is a brother."

"Yes," said Chantal to Valentin, obediently changing to the second person singular, "you don't often talk about Madagascar."

"If you're interested," said Valentin to Chantal, addressing her likewise, "I'm quite willing."

Whereupon they both became pensively and intuitively mute.

"Well, what about it?" asked Julia, looking up, "aren't you going to have any more oysters?"

"Er," said Paul.

"You aren't going to let Valentin's funny jokes put you off your feed, are you?"

"Your little white wine is really amazing," said Paul.

"Don't talk nonsense! You surely aren't going to believe everything you hear, like peasants. In the first place, these little animals here—could be that they're alive now, but in half an hour they'll all be dead. Because the ones I haven't eaten, and the ones the maid hasn't eaten, and I warn you we've got to leave her some, well, they'll be chucked in the garbage can. And if that happens, it'll take them even longer to croak, the poor little things. Isn't that even more cruel?"

"There's some truth in what you say," said Paul, who didn't take much convincing.

Chantal was still hesitating.

"You might just as well have the benefit of them," Julia told her. "They'll only go to waste."

All three, then, gave themselves up once again to the absorption of raw mollusks. While Valentin tried to take his mind off things by scratching the tip of his nose with his fork, the others devoted so much ardor to their cannibalism that they had to make a great effort of will in order to leave a few for the maid. A heavy haze of happiness settled once more over the room.

Picking at an interstice between two teeth with the nail of her index finger, Julia asks the Batagras, in a negligent voice:

"And Marinette? How's she getting on? Still as much of a bitch?"

X

THEY'D INVITED some of the local tradespeople in for coffee, it was indispensable. Julie had even considered getting the funeral procession to follow a long and complicated route through the twelfth arrondissement to make a bit of publicity, but they'd given up the idea on account of the expense. M. and Mme. Panneton, M. and Mme. Balustre, M. and Mme. Verterelle, M. and Mme. Poucier, piled into the Brûs' salon, as well as M. Houssette and M. Virole who had come on their own, apologizing for the absence of their ladies who were unable to attend on housewifely or storekeeperly grounds.

The choir sang Nanette's praises, and the most solecistic among them even added those of Meussieu Chignole, but the Brû family either abstained from piping up or piped up pretty imperceptibly. Julia was once again overcome by lachrymose convulsions, which they decided to calm by not saying another word about the deceased and by covering her memory with the loam of well-bred silence.

Julie, choking back her sobs with the same decision as she had knocked back the oysters, suggests a glass of brandy.

"R isn't any," says Valentin, "I'll go get some."

"Oh, don't bother," yelps the choir, which considers that the Brû household is not well run.

"Oh but of course," Julia insists, and thinks: have to know how to make sacrifices.

"I won't be a minute," says Valentin.

"I'll come with you," says Paul.

They took their hats and, on the stairs, Valentin confided his quandary to his brother-in-law:

"I don't know whether I ought to go to Houssette's or to Virole's. Whatever I do, I'm going to offend one of them."

"Buy two bottles, stupid, one from each of them."

"That's all very well," murmured Valentin, "but I haven't got enough money."

"Are you trying to touch me?"

"No, I mean it. I must have just about enough."

"Does Julia give you your pocket money every morning?"

"Every week. I had a supplement this morning for the tips to the undertakers, the car, the bottle of port, and the bottle of brandy. But not for two bottles of brandy."

"Tell you what," said Paul, in an extreme state of euphoria, "I'll stand one."

"That's an idea," said Valentin.

They went to Madame Houssette's, greeted her extremely politely, and Paul bought a bottle of Courvoisier, then they went to Madame Virole's, which establishment comprised not only a grocer's but also a bar counter. Madame Virole only sold one brand of brandy, and it was one that Paul didn't know. He insisted on tasting it. Even though his stomach had been devastated by the water of Lake Tsimanampetsotsa, Valentin couldn't refuse to keep him company.

"Very good," said Paul approvingly. "A bottle, Madame Virole, and we'll have the same again. Don't argue, lad. It's true—I could almost be your father."

"Why almost?" asked Valentin.

And, turning to the proprietress:

"People are never almost fathers; they either are or they aren't, isn't that true, Madame Virole?"

"Of course it's true! It's like deceived husbands! They either are, or they aren't."

78

"Oh, excuse me!" Paul protested. "There *is* such a thing as being almost deceived."

"Oh, you!" exclaimed Madame Virole, "I know your sort, you're going to come out with some kind of filth."

"Filth is a part of life," declared Paul, "and I maintain that it's possible to be an almost-deceived husband."

"He's an almostist," Valentin ventured, hoping to get Madame Virole to appreciate him.

But she took not the slightest notice.

"Oh, shut up, you," said Broubaillat. "You can't talk, you're almost a virgin."

"What did I say," murmured Valentin.

"Now take me for example," Paul went on, "sometimes I'm completely deceived, and then at other times I'm only almost deceived."

"Ha ha ha," said Madame Virole.

"The same again, Madame Virole."

"Not for me," said Valentin. "I'll take the bottle and go home with it."

"There's no great hurry," Paul grumbled.

He knocked back the two glasses of the third round.

"How much is that?" he stammered.

"With the bottle?" asked Madame Virole.

"Of course."

Valentin was waiting for him at the door.

"Come on, get a move on, almost-father," said Valentin, dragging him out.

"Did you answer my question concerning the rhododendronization of the Malagasy plateaus?"

"Of course."

"Then you agree with me?"

"Absolutely."

"Then you're a brother."

"In-law."

"A brother-in-law is a brother. Personally, I'm all for relationships by marriage."

"There's something to be said for them."

"Well then, if you're a brother, Chantal's your sister."

"In-law," replied Valentin, whose temperance was somewhat disturbed by the two brandies.

"So you see," said Paul, "if you were to make a pass at Chantal, it'd be incest."

"Out of the question."

Paul stopped Valentin in order to collapse on his shoulder, weeping:

"Don't incest too much, Valentin, don't incest too much."

Valentin dragged him a few steps further.

"We're there," said Valentin.

Paul pulled out his handkerchief and wiped his eyes. Then he gave his nose a good blow.

"That's better," he said.

When they went in, they were greeted by protestations:

"You certainly took your time," said Julia, frowning with anguish at the sight of two bottles.

"Mesdames Virole and Houssette wish to be remembered to you," said Valentin to Houssette and Virole.

The two latter immediately understood the allusion and promised themselves that they would reserve their custom for such a gentlemanly young man as Meussieu Brû. Meussieu Brû sold frames for miniatures and photographs. Meussieu Chignole, his predecessor, had only gone in for frames for miniatures; a small-time craftsman in the Faubourg Saint-Martin had worked exclusively for him. However, the decadence of this art, that of the miniature, a decadence which had begun with the discovery of printing, whose date cannot be fixed with any precision, at least in the Occident, but which is certainly anterior to the second half of the fifteenth century, and to which the finishing touches were put by the discovery of photography which goes back to the year eighteen hundred and thirty-nine, had singularly limited the clientèle of Meussieu Chignole. The Popular Front was the last straw for him, as his craftsman joined a trade union and started charging him at rates which represented a considerable increase on those he had been asking ever since the year eighteen hundred and ninety-two. This betrayal disgusted Chignole and contributed no little to hastening the death of the said citizen.

When Valentin took over the business under Nanette's guidance, he took to the miniature and its frames without any great surprise. But the supplier, stricken with acute old age, now only turned out three or four frames a year, which would not have sufficed to support three people plus the possible children. Nanette was then all for launching out into modernity, in other words, photograph frames. Photograph frames did in fact justify hopes of a considerably vaster clientèle than that which was still having itself miniaturized. Valentin, then, resorted to the best manufacturers, such as Messrs. Léon Leville, and he was thus enabled to offer amateurs the purest specimens of the genuine Paris novelty, the fanciest of fancy goods. Soon the entire twelfth arrondissement would be framing their loves and their memories chez Valentin Brû, rue de la Brèche-aux-Loups. "Valentin Brû, framer to Rabelais," said his trade cards, and this turn of phrase impressed the populace from the Gare de Lyon to the Porte Dorée. Valentin would have liked to have circulated it even more widely by other means, and especially by means of the animated cartoons for which you had to ring Balzac double-0-0-one, but Nanette had dissuaded him on account of the expense.

He got up at six in the morning and made his own breakfast, for at six o'clock the cleaning woman who was called a maid hadn't yet arrived. Then he went downstairs and removed the wooden shutters, though still without opening the store. For a while he watched the folk going to work, then he went upstairs again to wash and dress. In this way he managed to get up to half-past seven. Then he lay down again on his bed fully clothed and went back to sleep until eight o'clock. Julia, on the days when she got up early, was vaguely opening her eyes. She demanded her breakfast which was brought to her by the monster, who had arrived in the meantime. Then Valentin went down again to the florist's on the corner and bought a rose or a bunch of violets which he put in a little glazed vase on the cash desk, this made a good impression, and, this time, well and truly opened, on the stroke of nine, his store that sold frames for miniatures and photographs.

He had provided all the persons present with the wherewithal to show to the best advantage the mugs of their forebears or their brats. Even the Babagras could see the different stages in Marinette's life immobilized between two sheets of glass held together by a metal clasp. On the other hand the

Pannetons and the Ponciers, for example, still fancied the flowery bronze effect that placed the portrayed person in an immediately artistic surround.

Having drunk their glass of spirits, the local tradesmen began to withdraw with many polite expressions which didn't stop them thinking their private thoughts. Thanks to Julia they were taking away with them enough material to nourish the comments of many a vigil. Her colorful language and the scurrilous nature of her stories had amazed them. For up to the present they had hardly known her; she didn't often appear in the store; this new trade, which was not hers, left her completely cold.

Being members of the family, Chantal and Paul were the last to leave. They all agreed that they would have a bite together soon. At the Batrugas'.

"And Marinette must have dinner with us," said Julia. "Anyone might think you were trying to keep her out of my sight."

The Butragas made no objection, it was easier to think up an excuse on the evening. Then there were kisses all round. Watching Valentin lightly brushing Chantal's pink, powderized cheeks with his modest, chaste lips, Jules hummed "not on the mouth," a song from his youth, which made Julia laugh good-naturedly.

The Butagras' steps could be heard going down the stairs.

"Out of the question, eh," said Julia, pouring herself out a glass of brandy.

The Bugratas could be heard slamming the street door.

"What's out of the question?" asked Valentin, looking sadly at the coffee cups, ravaged with lipstick or weltering in ash.

The Batratras' steps could be heard receding.

"You gallivanting with Chantal," said Julia.

"Oooh," said Valentin, dismayed. "It certainly is out of the question, as you say."

"The way they go on about it, they'll end up putting the idea into your head. Or into your tail. I don't mind betting that the reason Paul wanted to go out with you was to chat about that."

"Quite true," admitted Valentin, surprised.

"What did he say?"

"He was drunk."

"Tell me."

Valentin rubs one side of his head with the flat of his hand.

"He said that sometimes he was completely deceived, and other times only almost."

"You see, he's pushing you into it."

"What's he pushing me into?"

"And then what? What else did he say?"

Valentin was wondering, he'd forgotten, but to please Julia he replied:

"He said that Chantal's boobs, they're like this."

And he made a gesture indicating firmness.

Julia slapped her thigh:

"What a laugh, they dangle right down to her navel."

She cackled. Then, abruptly:

"By the way, what about the bottles of brandy? Did you pay for them?"

"One each," replied Valentin, deciding to buy himself a piggy bank, or else open an account with a savings bank.

But, for the savings bank, maybe you need your spouse's permission.

"What are you thinking about?"

Julia was carefully studying his physiognomy. She concluded:

"He paid for them both, eh?"

"He wasn't as drunk as all that."

Isn't lying nasty, Valentin was thinking, while Julia seemed to be preoccupied by other problems.

"Do you believe in table-turning?" she suddenly asked.

"I don't know."

"Madame Verterelle told me that it wasn't just a lot of nonsense."

"And what d'you get out of it?"

"You can communicate with the dead."

"Ah."

Valentin shrank.

"We could communicate with Nanette," Julie went on. "She could give you some advice."

She looked at him:

"You don't like the idea?"

83

"Not much."

"Why not?"

"Just don't like it. In Madagascar, for example . . ."

"You get on my nerves, you and your Madagascar. We aren't in Madagascar, we're in Paris. We'll try. You can do that to please me, can't you?"

"Of course," said Valentin, who much preferred table-turning to oysters.

"Go and get the little table from the bedroom, then. Madame Verterelle told me that it was just right."

"You don't think it's a bit soon after Nanette's death? It might disturb her."

"On the contrary: being so recent, it'll be all the nicer."

Valentin brought in the little table, then, and, on his own initiative, closed the shutters.

"What do we have to do?"

"We put our hands like this. And then we wait."

Valentin put his hands like that, and then waited.

"Anyone there?" asked Julia, in a rather disconcerting voice. The table raised itself and rapped once.

"You see, there *is* someone," Julia murmured, deeply moved. "We'll ask him some questions. You count the number of raps, that gives you the letters of the alphabet."

"It must be never-ending," said Valentin.

"Shut up."

Raising her head up toward the ceiling, her eyes closed, she said in a deep voice:

"Spirit, what's your name?"

Twelve raps replied.

"L," said Valentin and Julia together, having counted on their fingers.

"That isn't a name," added Valentin.

"Shut up."

Five raps followed.

"E," they observed.

Then eight.

"H!"

Then twenty-one.

"I thought it was never going to stop," said Valentin.

The table danced up and down.

"You see, you're making it impatient with your impatience," said Julia.

"In any case, it isn't Nanette."

"We'll see."

With a perseverance that she wouldn't have applied to any other enterprise, Julie finally obtained the name of Nanette's substitute: *Le Hussard Brû.*

"He's sure to be an ancestor," said Valentin.

"*You* ask him," said Julia, offended that the table had chosen the Brû family in preference to hers.

"Am I one of your descendants?" asked Valentin.

"The son of my great-grandson."

"Hello, Grandfather," said Valentin.

"Hello, young 'un," replied the table.

"He's got an Alsatian accent, your ancestor," whispered Julie.

"What regiment of hussars were you in?" asked Valentin.

"First of all in the ninth. I fought at Jena with Lannes' army, under the orders of General Treilhard."

"And what did you do that day?"

"With drawn sword, I was responsible for the seriousness of German philosophy."

"Well, that at least," said Valentin.

"Good evening," said the table, from which they could subsequently extract nothing whatsoever.

Valentin opened the windows again. He apologized:

"I didn't know I had an ancestor who fought at Jena on the 14th of October, 1806."

"How d'you know it was that day?"

"I read it on a tear-off calendar," he replied prudently.

"In any case, we won't be talking to your forefather again," declared Julie.

"Oh, personally you know," said Valentin.

"I do know," said Julia. "What can we do now?" she added, yawning.

"I wouldn't mind opening the store, but that would give us a bad reputation. Would you like to go to the movies?"

"To see a load of rubbish? No thanks. Like that thing you took me to see last time which was so screwy. What was it called again?"

"*Modern Times.*"

"That's right. Your Charlie Chaplin, I can't stand him. And anyway, it wouldn't be decent on a day of mourning."

"Let's go and see a sad film, then," suggested Valentin.

"If it gets about in the neighborhood that I went to the movies on the day of my mother's funeral, there'd be talk."

"Well, better not then," said Valentin conciliatorily.

"Yes but the neighbors? I don't give a fuck for what they think. In no wise, by no means, and not at all. Only, let's go and see something good. Is *The Vivandière's Three Lovers* on anywhere?

"No," said Valentin firmly.

"Pass me the paper. Huh! What did I tell you? There's even a big ad. At the Rex. It's lovely at the Rex, with the organ and the sky and everything. You feel as if you're floating on air."

"Do you really like stories about soldiers?"

"What a laugh you are. You're as proud as anything that your old ancestor was a swashbuckler and yet you don't want to go and see the present-day ones."

Valentin yielded, and went to comb his hair: the Rex, oh my goodness.

Julie put her shoes back on.

In the hall, she noticed a scarf. One of the Assembly of Notables, or his wife, had left it behind.

"D'you know whose this is?"

"No," said Valentin. "Maybe it's Madame Verterelle's. That's right, it's Madame Verterelle's."

"We'll drop it in on our way," said Julia. "They'll appreciate that."

"Good idea."

Julia picked up the scarf, and then she saw a street which must have been a Paris street, but she hardly knew Paris. A lady was walking in front of her, without the slightest doubt Madame Verterelle. All of a sudden she collapsed. People ran up. And Julia knew that she was dead.

Valentin turned and looked at her:

"What's the matter?"

She didn't answer.

"Would you rather stay at home? And not go to the Rex?"
he asked, full of hope.

"We'll drop in at Madame Verterelle's and give her back
her handkerchief, and then we'll go and see *The Vivandière's Lovers*. I'm sure it's a film Nanette would have liked."

XI

"Good morning, Madame. Lovely day, isn't it? my goodness,
summer will soon be here. Is it for a miniature or a photograph? A photograph. And what size? You don't know? Have
you got the photo with you? No? Then, dear Madame, how do
you expect me to sell you a frame? You want to choose it just
like that? Just by guesswork? That's a grave mistake, Madame.
You'll choose it either too big or too small. My motto, Madame, is that the customer must be satisfied. I don't go in for
anything amateurish. The frame must be the indisputable
complement of the photograph. It would be a crime to put the
likeness of a loved one in just anything. For it *is* a loved one
whose . . . ? Your son? You see. If we had the exact size, I
would suggest this one which has a very young look about it.
For he is a very young boy, isn't he? A young mother can
only have a young son . . . but of course, but of course . . .
Thirteen? And does he already know what he wants to be?
Ah! An engineer. That's a fine profession. To make lightweight
motorcycles, corkscrews, dams. It seems we need them badly,
dams, to keep out the Pacific. Would you like to take this
frame, it's quite the latest fashion. If it doesn't go with the
photo of your young Pierre, sorry, Jean, just bring it back. I'll
exchange it for you. Oh but not at all, Madame, it's only nat-

ural. That'll be nineteen francs ninety-five. Perhaps, Madame, you would care to leave me your address. I'll send you my catalogue and let you know if I have any new articles that might interest you. Let me write it down: Madame Lormier, 12 rue de Madagascar, ah, I know it. It isn't far away? My goodness, it all depends on what you mean by that. No, *I* thank *you*. Good-by, Madame."

"Good morning, Madame Foucet. I'll bet it's for your young lady's first communion photo. There, you see, I guessed. I say young lady because, well, isn't she big for her age. She's already started her . . . ? Aha, aha. And everything went all right? She was very upset? You ought to have warned her, Madame Foucet, it's a mother's duty. There's not a single number of *Marie-Claire* that doesn't recommend it. That's the little curse of the second sex, as you might say. You haven't got the photo with you? But Madame Foucet, I don't want to sell you a frame haphazard! I wouldn't be much good at my trade if I did that. You think you've got the size in your mind's eye, but you'll see, Madame Foucet, you'll take one that's either too big or too small. If it's too big, the photo swims in it, and if it's too small you have to cut it, and that's a crime. Come back tomorrow with a proof, then, Madame Foucet. Ah, you'd have liked to have it this evening? I understand your impatience. Why don't you take two? A big one and a little one. The other will always come in handy. Or I could exchange it. These two? I quite agree with you: they look pure and radiant. That'll be forty-one francs 05, and we'll forget about the five centimes! No, *I* thank *you*."

"Good morning, Meussieu. For a miniature or a photo? A photo. Parents? sisters? your fiancée? Yes, that *is* my business, Meussieu, that certainly is my business, I'm not going to sell you just anything. You're young. You're nineteen. Twenty, sorry. Last April the 14th. But . . . aren't you Meussieu Houssette's nephew? I thought as much. There's a family resemblance. Your mother is Meussieu Houssette's sister? Ah, she married his brother. Then your name is Housette. It's a nice name, not very common. Have you any brothers and sisters? One sister. Fine, fine. Your uncle is a friend. You can tell me in complete confidence. Is it for your girlfriend's photo? No? Well then? You understand, Meussieu Pierre, sorry, Jean, that I can't help you choose if I don't know who the frame is going to frame. A racing cyclist? Lapébie? Ah, he's great. He's got a future, that lad. Quite capable of winning the Tour de France. You've got his photo? Good, good. You're the ideal customer. Here, what about this exclusive little model from Léon Leville and Co., that would be just the thing: a bicycle in white metal and we stick the photo in the front wheel which is designed for that very purpose, the price of the glass is included, the back wheel stays just as it is. You like it? Maybe a bit expensive? We can come to an arrangement, I'll wrap it up for you. Here. Well, that's thirty francs, too much? Pay me half today, and you can give me the rest tomorrow or the day after. No no, that'll be quite all right. Fifteen francs, no, *I* thank *you*. But look, you've got fifteen francs left. To go out with this evening? Believe me, we always have to pay our debts, that's the way we get rich. After that you can forget about it. And fifteen make thirty. No, *I* thank *you*. Good-by, Meussieu Pierre. And up Lapébie!"

"Good morning, Madame. Madame . . . ? Madame Gache. Ah! that's right. So this one is too big? Nothing simpler, we'll exchange it. And the photo? You've left it in. Phew, what a good-looking young man. An Adonis. Meussieu your husband? Don't blush, Madame, I'm what you might call a father confessor, as silent as the tombstone and as discreet as the newspapers. Quite true, it does sort of float, your photo. I'll find you something better. Here, this one, highly recommended by *Marie-Claire*. Would you allow me to insert this gentleman between two sheets of glass? What an effect, eh? You'll take it, then? It's a bit more expensive than the other one, that doesn't frighten you? Will I take the other one back? But of course. Thirty-two francs 95 for this one minus sixteen francs 10, that comes to . . . You paid twenty-five francs for it? But excuse me, Madame, look at this, there's a scratch. You can't see it? It's very obvious, though. There. Here. This object is slightly damaged. I'd take it back to do you a favor, but in your own interests I'd advise you to keep it, you're sure to have a bigger photo one day that'll fit it. I think that's good advice. Well then we said thirty-two francs 95. Here, I'll forget about the centimes and let you have it for thirty-three francs. That was just a joke. And five centimes which make thirty-three, and two thirty-five, and fifteen fifty, no, *I* thank *you*."

There are also the slack periods, quite long enough for wiping, cleaning, and filing. Valentin does everything himself, even the store windows. And with all this, he still has time on his hands. Work on the other sort of cleaning (fingernails, ears) can be prolonged in a manner undreamed of by those who have insufficiently studied the question. But in spite of everything, there is a limit. Valentin is sorry he can't give himself a pedicure; he tried twice, but he noticed that both times he missed a sale. One mustn't make hasty generalizations, but it does rather seem that a de-shoed and de-socked tradesman crouching over his dogs puts himself in an inferior position vis-à-vis his customer. So then Valentin decided to go in for reading. But what? And how? If you wait for your customers with your nose stuck in a newspaper, that makes rather a bad impression. With your nose stuck in a book, that's even stranger. Valentin adopts a well-known solution: to slide the work or the publication into a file with the inscription in nice round handwriting: Bills. Only you mustn't let yourself be too carried away by your reading. And even supposing that there is an answer to the question of how, there still remains the question of what. Valentin doesn't feel attracted by anything in particular. There are the new books recommended by the news sheets, but they cost quite a bit, anything up to twelve or fifteen francs. There are the old authors, and these you can easily find in the public library, but there are so many of them. Which ones to start with? Should you go down the centuries or up the generations? Valentin adopts a concrete method: he chooses the nearest ones, that's to say those who have a street named after them in the twelfth arrondissement: Charles Baudelaire, Taine, Diderot, Ledru-Rollin, for example. Unfortunately, the public library in the twelfth arrondissement doesn't possess a single work by Ledru-Rollin; this setback discourages Valentin. In the meantime, he's thought of something else: he'll study for his *baccalauréat*. Not by correspondence, that would cost money, but on his own. He communicates his project to Julia, who immediately discovers the seventeen necessary and sufficient reasons to prove the futility of such an undertaking. Valentin acknowledges it.

There remains the possibility of handicrafts. He could go in for carpentry, locksmithery—or even frame-making! He would create a new style, he'd have individualized models, he'd make them to order. Only, there's no room. He gave up this idea all the more easily in that he already knew it. But the problem remained. One day he'd tried out the solution that consists in shutting up shop and leaving a little note: "Back in five minutes," and then going and mucking about here and there for an hour, but he had heard that Madame Mentonnet, the dry-cleaner, one of the ones they hadn't asked in for coffee, had turned up while he was out and had declared that she wasn't going to put herself out another time for nothing, and that he, Meussieu Brû, would be extremely lucky if he ever got her, Madame Mentonnet's, business again.

At seven o'clock, they shut up shop. Valentin takes the handle out of the door and makes his getaway. He doesn't put the shutters up until around nine o'clock, after dinner. At five past seven he goes into the Café des Amis, in the rue de Wattignies. He prefers it to all the other bistros in the neighborhood because of its name. He doesn't sit down, he stays at the counter, he shakes various mitts and is served with a Dubonnet without having to ask for it. He has abandoned his *vin blanc gommé* for this drink which is equally healthy but has more zip. People talk, he listens. He does talk a bit, too, so as not to seem distant. They discuss the Expo 37, which may well not open because of the strikes, but which will be good for trade if it does open. They discuss Spain and the Popular Front, but with moderation. Above all they discuss cycling, football, and the improvement of the equine species. Valentin nods, smiles, repeats some cliché he's read in the paper and which in general is very particularly appreciated, which always surprises Valentin, because after all, the others read the paper too, don't they? Finally they come down to discussing the petty occurrences of the neighborhood; these are the only ones that interest Julia.

"How much today?" she asks him.

"Two hundred and thirty-four francs. A marvelous day."

"What can have got into people, having themselves framed like that?" she mutters, stashing the cash away.

"That's nothing. You'll see, when the Expo's on."

"Another load of crap, their Expo; it'll never open."

"They say it will."

"You'll see. You're just as much of a sucker as your buddies in the bistro. What were they saying today?"

Valentin polishes off the remains of his vegetable soup, a substantial brew as thick as glue. He licks his chops. Then he starts cutting his bread into cubes.

"Madame Verterelle has kicked the bucket," he announces. "In the street. She was walking along when all of a sudden, pff, she had a stroke, she went sprawling, they picked her up off the pavement, she was dead."

Valentin takes the plates and goes to bring in the next course, the remains of the stew they'd had for lunch.

"I wonder whether she's going to stick herself in a table, now, and come and have a little chat with us."

Valentin hasn't the slightest objection to eating the same thing at dinner as at lunch. On the contrary. In the evening, it's been simmering longer, stewing longer, in short, it's more to his taste. He alternates the absorption of bits of mutton with that of little slabs of bread well soaked in gravy. From time to time, a great gulp of wine adds variety to the different flavors. Why, actually, is he taking such a very special delight in this tonight? He wonders about this vaguely, but fortunately doesn't find an answer to the question until his plate has been wiped so clean that it would be wasting water to wash it.

Raising his eyes, the strange sight that he perceives leaves him for a few moments open-mouthed. Julia is not eating. The stew is stagnating on her plate, instead of being shoveled down her digestive tube.

"Don't you like it?" asks an incredulous Valentin.

And as she doesn't answer, he puts forward another hypothesis, which is equally improbable:

"It isn't old mother Verterelle's death that's got you into such a state, is it?"

"You wouldn't understand," she replies abruptly, and throws herself on the grub, causing it to disappear in the twinkling of an eye. "Tell me more," she says, wiping her mouth, while Valentin brings the cheese and the cookies.

"I don't know any more. They're going to bury her tomorrow."

"At Reuilly?"

"No, at Bagneux."

"We'll go, of course."

"Someone's got to look after the store. You'd better go on your own."

"I'd rather not."

"I'm not going to shut for another whole morning."

"You could get an apprentice. Unpaid. We'd just give him his lunch."

"I don't know if we could, what with the new welfare laws."

"Poof, what do we care about them, the Popular Front and its laws."

"In any case, I don't need anyone."

"How many people have you seen today?"

"Four. Madame Foucet, Houssette's nephew, a lady who lives in the rue de Madagascar, there's a coincidence for you."

"Why?" says Julia.

"Just like that. And then a Madame Gache who brought me back a frame for an exchange."

"I hope you didn't exchange anything."

"No, of course not."

"And what did they all say?"

"Houssette's nephew is twenty, has a sister, and likes bicycle racing. He brought me Lapébie's portrait."

"Who's he?"

"A cycling champion that he wanted to frame. He's not a bad-looking boy, the nephew, dark brown hair, brown eyes, oval face. Special peculiarity: the first phalanx of his left-hand index finger is deformed. Does that interest you?"

"It might. And the Foucet woman?"

"Ah, her, her little girl has made her first communion. She's already started the curse . . ."

"She's had one all her life, in her mother," Julia sneered.

"Madame Gache brought me the portrait of her boyfriend. A gigolo."

"And her, what's she like?"

"Oh, great."

Valentin was wary of too lyrical descriptions; otherwise he'd have said: a fabulous dame, getting on a bit, with boobs out to here."

"That's vague: 'great.' "

"She was blonde. But artificial in my opinion, the blonde."

"How old?"

Valentin scratched the tip of his nose. Questions of age were always difficult to deal with in Julia's presence.

He ventured:

"Thirty."

"How was she dressed?"

"She had a coat, I think."

"What color?"

"I didn't notice. She had a ring with a ruby, and she was wearing a wedding ring."

"That's not enough for me to recognize her by," said Julia pensively.

"Why would you need to recognize her?" asked Valentin, amazed.

Julia didn't answer.

Valentin dunked his biscuits in his wine; the great art consists in leaving them in just long enough for them to be well and truly impregnated, but not so long that they disintegrate in the glass just when you want to take them out. This absorbing occupation didn't allow Valentin to see the charming smile Julia was bestowing on him.

A kick in the tibia reminds him to pay more attention.

"I like it," says Julia, "when you tell me things about people. It's very sweet of you."

"Really? It doesn't bore you?"

He observed, with some despair, that his petit beurre had begun to dissolve.

"Only you ought to give me more details. Be more precise. Describe people properly. Can't you get photos of your customers?"

"Don't see how."

"And your pals in the bistro, don't they confide in you?"

"I don't know them all that well."

"One or two more aperitifs, that'll get them chatting. But don't you talk. Whatever you do, don't ever talk!"

"So you're driving me to drink now, are you?"

"'Course not, my precious, you just have to understand."

"Understand what?"

Julia didn't answer.

"What have you got at the back of your mind?" Valentin asked her.

"The back of my chair," replied Julia, who wasn't very tall, and who was sitting in an armchair.

XII

Sunday was the most difficult day; they'd resigned themselves to the movies and, so as not to argue about which to choose, they always went to the same one; all the more so as Meussieu Crampon, the manager, always reserved two seats for them.

"What's got into Chantal," grumbled Julia. "A Sunday! Inviting us to tea! She's nuts. And it would have to be the very day when Tarzan's on."

"Yes, certainly our unlucky day," acquiesced Valentin who, personally, was delighted to be going to a tea party.

He believed that tea parties were something that only existed in *Marie-Claire*.

Having changed metros only twice, they got to the Butugras'.

"There's something fishy going on," said Julia. "You'll see."

"Makes a change, a tea party," said Valentin trying to be conciliatory. "And we'll still be hungry enough for the tripe tonight."

"My foot," said Julia. "Anything they venture to offer me, I shall eat it."

"All the more tripe for me," said Valentin.

"Maybe they want to borrow some money from us."

"They don't look as if they were pushed for an odd franc or two."

"Don't count on it. Government employees are always hard up. And their wives even more so. I know my Chantal."

"What'll we do if they try and touch us?"

"Pff, that's not difficult: what with the taxes and all the regular payments, we haven't got a bean to bless ourselves with."

"And then there's the gas bill," remarked Valentin.

"Don't mix everything. The taxes and the regular ones will be enough. Got it?"

"And just look at this year's taxes, it's even worse than last year. What's staring us in the face?"

"Very good. The welfare laws are all very fine, but it's the bureaucrats who profit by them and the storekeepers who pay."

"Very good. I think we're prepared," said Valentin optimistically.

"And don't let yourself be bamboozled by your girlfriend."

"What girlfriend?"

They rang. A young person pleasantly disguised as a soubrette came and opened the door to them. Julia looked at her with a severe eye.

"Hm, that's new," said she. "Have you been here long, my girl?"

"A week, Madame."

"They're nuts," sighed Julia.

After she had relieved them of their outer and upper garments, the young person pleasantly disguised as a soubrette opened a door and indicated the way.

"We know, we know," grumbled Julie. "I was here before you."

Chantal was waiting for them, alone. Valentin shoots a rapid glance around and about, trying to spot the teacups and the petits fours, but perceives nothing of the sort. They would be brought in later, no doubt. There weren't any other guests, either, nor any bridge tables. He had tried to learn how to play bridge on his own but hadn't managed it, and he'd given it up when he had realized that no one in his neighborhood knew how to play that particular game.

"You're not with us, Valentin," said Chantal, kissing him.

She looked very affable today; anything but a vamp.

"Here," Julia began, "who the hell's that tart who opened the door to us?"

"She's a maid."

"You'll see what she'll cost you. Not just her wages. Tut tut, I don't even want to know how much you pay her. What's more, it's quite obvious from the look of her that she belongs to a trade union. And what about her benefits, they're going to add up."

"Oh I don't know, you can't say it's not convenient."

"And wasn't your cleaning woman enough?"

"I'm keeping her on as well."

Her face convulsed, her eyes ready to burst out of their sockets and land on the floor with the flabby sound of marbles made of offal, Julia turned to Valentin and bellowed:

"The bastards! They must have won the lottery!"

Chantal laughed heartily, without malice.

"Oh no," she said, "oh no."

On the table there was a little copper bell with a long handle of the same material. She picked it up and swung it with a gracious movement. The merry, sparkling sound which ensued delighted Valentin and gave him renewed hope.

The young person pleasantly disguised as a soubrette appeared toot sweet; and still as smiling.

"Catherine, have you informed Meussieu that our guests have arrived?"

"Yes, Madame."

"Then, Catherine, you may bring the tea and the petits fours. And some port for the messieux, if they prefer it."

"Which bottle of port shall I select, Madame?"

"Well, Catherine, you can bring the Sandeman 1878."

"Very good, Madame."

Julia had listened to this dialogue in silence, her mouth half open and her face marked with all the stigmata of the most hideous stupidity.

"Well, Valentin, how's business?" asked Chantal airily, turning to him.

Valentin, whom the Chantal-Catherine dialogue had on the contrary moved to enthusiasm, replied fervently:

"Fine! Just fine! I took in two hundred and sixty-one francs yesterday, plus one false five franc piece. It's rare for anyone to manage to palm one off on me. Hm, I could have shown it to Paul, it might have interested him."

"I don't think that comes within his province," said Chantal with an extremely kind smile, "and in any case he won't be interested in such things much longer."

Julia, whom all these remarks reached through layer upon layer of cotton wool and fog, on hearing the last words uttered by her sister, very slowly raised her eyebrows. Whereupon in pranced Paul, all primped and preened.

"How are you, dear sister," he cried in a false voice, "how are you, my dear Valentin."

Meanwhile Catherine and the cleaning lady were between them bringing in four trays. The quantity and variety of the petits fours, and also the quality of the material of Paul's new suit, increased Julia's confusion and she thought she was going mad.

"I'll try some tea," Valentin replied to one of the questions he had been asked, "I've never had any."

As for the petits fours! Would he care for one! The first that melted in his mouth confirmed him in his optimistic mood. He kept picking out different ones, because there was plenty of variety, that was what was amusing.

"How's your business?" Paul asked him.

"Terrific. I took in two hundred and sixty-one francs yesterday, plus one false five franc piece. I was just asking Chantal if it wouldn't interest you to see it."

"No. Money is the only part of the metric system that didn't come within my province. For I must add that, for the last two weeks, it is I who no longer come within the province of the weights and measures."

Julia, whose conduct up till now had been that of one hit over the head by a bludgeon, Julia took the floor and, in a mournful voice, asked hopefully:

"Did they throw you out?"

"No, I resigned."

She grabbed a handful of petits fours and started liquidating them; the biscuity ones she rapidly ground to pulp, the other ones, first she sucked up the cream, and then swallowed the surrounding pastry, projecting it into the nether regions of her gullet with a little backward flick of her tongue.

"And Marinette?" she asked, determined not to take any more notice of Paul, "aren't we going to see her?"

"She's out for a walk with her nanny," replied Chantal nonchalantly. "A glorious Danish girl who doesn't know a word of French. It's charming."

"You'll tire your man out if you get him too many beautiful girls," said Julia, who'd had enough of being impressed.

"It isn't difficult to keep a husband faithful if you surround him with nothing but monsters."

"Everyone her own method," retorted Julia.

Valentin, embarrassed, looked at Paul and smiled stupidly at him.

"Don't take any notice," said Paul easily. "That's the women's department—nothing to do with us. A cigar, Valentin?"

Julia grabbed the cigar case as it passed her, felt its leather, and suddenly she saw a busy workshop, conveyor belts, workbenches, workmen working, a picture from *Two Little Alsatians' Tour of France*, a book she had read as a child, before the 1914 war; but the wheels were turning, the men were moving, she even thought she could hear the sound of all this activity. Then everything disappeared, while Valentin was saying:

"No thanks. I might smoke two or three cigarettes a day, but that's all."

Julia gave Paul back his case and said:

"Well then, tell us what you have to tell. It's obvious that you're itching to. So, just like that, you've resigned?"

"Yes, I'm abandoning government service."

"For industry," said Julia.

Startled, Paul looked at her and said in a frightened voice: "How d'you know that?"

"I don't know it."

"You've just said it."

"I guessed."

"Tell me how you know that," Paul repeated, trying to make his voice authoritative.

"Oh bloody hell," exclaimed Julia, "isn't anyone allowed to guess anything any more?"

Chantal looked at her sister curiously. As for Valentin, he had just discovered a new kind of petit four that he hadn't so far tried.

"Well," said Paul, disconcerted, "you guessed right. Yes, it's for industry. I've accepted a post as assistant manager . . ."

"Only assistant?" said Julia.

"With a firm that makes rifle butts."

"Rifle butts?" exclaimed Valentin, with admiration.

"Yes, rifle butts. In Châtellerault."

"Who on earth would want to buy *one* rifle butt?" asked Valentin.

"We sell them to rifle manufacturers," Paul answered.

"Can't they make their own rifle butts?"

"We're specialists."

"Well," exclaimed Valentin, "with the war that's on its way, you're going to be in the money."

"Don't talk about things you don't know anything about," said Julia. "There isn't going to be a war, and any minute now the rifle manufacturers are going to be in the shit, and Paul with them."

"You're forgetting," Paul told her, "that there can be wars elsewhere than in Europe and that, on the other hand, quite apart from wars, people use rifles all the time in activities such as game shooting and the police force."

"Even so," said Valentin obstinately, "it's especially with the war that's on its way that you're going to be in the money."

"We already are in it," said Paul complacently. "If you want peace, prepare for war. We're re-arming."

"Oh well, that's different then," said Julia somewhat obscurely.

Like Valentin, she believed that people only made rifles once the wars had been declared.

"Even if there isn't a war, will you be able to sell your butts?" she asked, still not having altogether understood.

"Of course: we've got orders."

And, by pure chance, Paul managed to blow a smoke ring. He was triumphing on every level.

"And how did you get the job?"

"This isn't the first time that industrialists, estimating me at my true worth, have made me offers. Up till now, I've always refused. But this time, the bride was too beautiful for me to refuse to marry her."

He laughed complacently.

"It's like me," said Valentin seriously. "When I was offered a notions store, I didn't refuse it."

"You've got him a great job," said Julie to Chantal. "How much is he going to earn?"

"If I were to tell you," said Paul, "you wouldn't believe me."

"Tell just the same."

"The only trouble is," said Chantal, "that we're going to have to go and live in Châtellerault."

"That doesn't tell me how much he earns," said Julia.

"But we shall often come to Paris. With the car, it isn't far."

"What car?" asked Julia.

"An automobile car," replied Paul, in the most indifferent tone of voice he could muster.

"You're going to have a jalopy?"

"We were hesitating between a Citron and a Renault; in the end we decided on a Delage."

Julia raises her arms to the high heavens:

"They're nuts! You want to know what it is to throw money down the drain, Valentin? Well, have a look at them. Before six months are up they'll be coming to beg their bread outside our place."

"I hope you won't turn us away," said Chantal.

"No," said Julia. "I shall be so pleased to see you like that that I'll give you a slap-up meal and you'll be as sick as dogs, what with your shrunken beggars' stomachs that can't take decent folks' grub any more."

"In the meantime," said Paul, "let me invite *you* to have dinner with *me*."

"We don't mind if we do," said Julia. "We don't mind if we do."

"Aren't you afraid the tripe we had for lunch will go to waste?" Valentin asked her.

"Couldn't care less. We aren't going to refuse an invitation. Especially as Meussieu Brébragra wants to take us somewhere fancy. Isn't that right, Paul?"

"Eggsackly. I was thinking of taking you to the restaurant in the German pavilion at the Expo."

"You must be joking," said Valentin. "That's the most expensive. I read it in the paper."

"Let him do what he likes," said Julia. "He's got to spend his cash, he's got too much! And then, that way I'll get to see the Expo."

"Haven't you been yet?" asks Chantal.

"If you think I've got time!"

Valentin looks at her curiously. For some time now, as a matter of fact, he has been wondering what the hell she can do with herself all day long.

"Does your business take up a lot of your time?" asks Chantal.

"I suppose you think it runs itself? It isn't like a factory where the workers rush around like blue-assed flies while the bosses twiddle their thumbs."

"Here's our Julia gone all Popular Front," said Paul, laughing with exquisite good humor.

Catherine was removing the ravaged trays.

"Go and get us a taxi, will you," Chantal said to her.

"And what about your jalopy," said Julia, "the Delacrèmage."

"We haven't got it yet," said Chantal.

"You see," said Julie to Valentin. "They're already starting to climb down."

XIII

VALENTINE WAS giving his close attention to the soldier who was expounding the near and remote reasons for his apparition.

"You see," the soldier was saying, "I wasn't going to go and see the Expo without saying hello to my old pal Valentin. That just isn't done."

"That's decent of you," said Valentin, circumspectly. "I'm glad you haven't forgotten me."

"A buddy like you? Never!"

Valentin lowered his eyes modestly. The other inspected the premises with appreciative little nods.

"It's nice, here."

"I sweep it out every day," said Valentin proudly.

"You always liked that. You even wanted to be a street sweeper when you got your discharge."

"And I polish everything I can."

"So I see. It's all bright and shining. You've still got all the qualities of the private soldier."

"And I'm going to need them again soon."

"How come?"

Bourrelier seemed surprised.

"Well, for the next one," replied Valentin.

"A little bats, aren't you? Who d'you reckon we'll be fighting against?"

"Dunno," says Valentin prudently. "But I can feel it coming."

"What? War?"

"And how. And pronto."

"You know, having a trade doesn't seem to have made you very cheerful."

"Oh, that's got nothing to do with it! Nothing at all!"

And he laughed heartily.

"Listen," said Bourrelier, "we didn't go and stick our necks in the hornets' nest in Spain, did we? One less reason for war, right? And then, Hitler isn't crazy, he knows perfectly well that if he started a war he'd have a revolution on his hands, so you see, he isn't crazy. One day he'll go and tell Stalin where he gets off, but that's none of our business. So you see. And believe me, yours truly, he knows what he's talking about."

And he thrust his sleeve under the nose of ex-Private Brû.

"Hm," exclaimed the latter, "you've got one stripe less."

"Quite right, man. I've just been promoted to top sergeant."

"You're pleased, then."

"And how."

"You see, me, I'd never have made it," said Valentin.

Bourrelier gives him a great scap on the slapula.

"I should think not! But privates are needed, too, to defend France!"

Valentin considers this maxim worthy of examination, but Bourrelier doesn't give him time.

"By the way, you're one of the lucky ones. You were in the campaign against the Merina Hain-Tenys, so they can't recall you every so often like they can everyone else. It's in the *Official Gazette*. If they try it, you're allowed to object."

"What a lot of things you know," said Valentin. "You certainly deserve to be promoted some more. In the next one they may well make you a general."

"Risn't going to be a next one, I tell you!"

Valentin doesn't insist, and Bourrelier looks as if he doesn't know what to say any more.

"And," he adds. "And."

"Yes?" says Valentin.

"Are you on your own in the store?"

"As you see."

"And. And."

"Yes?" says Valentin.

"And Madame Brû?"

"Madame Brû is at home."

Valentin points to the ceiling.

"We live in the apartment above," he explains. "She hasn't time to bother with the store. I'm going to shut it, anyway, the store. Let's go and have a drink."

"Don't mind if I do," said Bourrelier.

"You'll see, we're going to a bistro you know."

"Not possible," said Bourrelier. "I've never been here before. It's the back of beyond, isn't it? I've got a pal who's a Parisian, when I told him I was going to see a pal who lived in the rue Brèche-aux-Loups, he wouldn't believe me."

"Well he's paying the penalty now," said Valentin.

"Good old Valentin. Come on, tell all. Marriage. Business. All that. Doing all right? Going well?"

"Not bad, not bad."

"That's vague: not bad."

"You'll have noticed that I haven't got a notions store any more."

"I have, I have. Personally I don't know the first thing about business, but can you make a living just selling frames?"

"You can see for yourself that I'm living, can't you? Here, talking about frames, I'll make you a present of one."

"Thanks."

"You see: the Café des Amis. Just like in le Bouscat."

"Sure. The Café des Amis, just like in le Bouscat. But it isn't the same. I don't know this one. What was that you were saying?"

"You've got very punctilious since you became a top sergeant," remarks Valentin.

"Apropos of the Café des Amis," says Bourrelier, "Didine's looking for a job in Paris. You wouldn't have anything for her, would you?"

"Oh la la, my missis wouldn't like that."

"Why not?"

"She's that jealous."

"Even so, if you can do something for Didine, she's a great girl."

"All right, tell her to come and see me. Maybe in the district."

They sit down and express their desires.

"Well well," remarks the top sergeant, "so you're drinking Dubonnet now. You'll see, you'll end up on Pernod. But let's come back to essentials. Well then, your better half, tell all. How d'you like conjugal bliss?"

"It's all right."

"Well, that's the main thing, then."

Forty seconds' silence.

"Well then," says Valentin, "so you've come to see the Expo."

"I didn't want to miss it. That's the sort of memories that never leave you."

"What did you especially like?"

"Give me time, I haven't been, yet."

"I got taken there a month ago."

"Then you can give me a few tips about what to see."

"There's so many things, you know. The Miniatures pavilion has its interest. The Photomontage section is worth visiting. Then there's the Palace of Frames, but that might well be a bit technical for you. Naturally I didn't miss the Madagascar pavilion, but I didn't recognize anything. I even began to wonder whether I'd ever set foot in the place. You'll see. Naturally, when the people with me asked me, I said 'That's exactly it,' or 'I certainly ought to remember that, didn't I,' and my brother-in-law even told me that it wasn't good grammar to say 'I didn't ought.' Did you know that, Top Sergeant?"

"'Course I did. Who d'you think you're talking to?"

"You see, my brother-in-law would tell you that you ought to say 'to whom.'"

"Look here, your brother-in-law, he's nothing but a stupid cunt."

"Don't worry about him, he's become an industrialist. He's not short of cash. He's the husband of the lady who came to interview you about me."

"I remember."

"What was I saying? Ah yes, so we were all four there at the Expo. Paul, Chantal, pretty name that don't you think, and Julia, that's my better half, and naturally they asked me to explain all this and that. For instance, what's the difference between a Sakalava* and a Hova.* Do *you* know?"

"I did once."

"Well, I didn't. Luckily, this bored everyone, so we moved on. After that we saw the Russian pavilion, which is really majestic and very interesting. For instance you can see a car, there, that they've made all by themselves."

"Are you becoming a Communist?"

"No but really, you'll see: a real car."

"Did you see it in action?"

"No."

"You see. It's all a fake. Nothing but a bit of metal. If you think that with their regime they're even capable of sticking a couple of screws together."

"How do you do that?" asked Valentin.

Bourrelier stepped back a pace or two, to see if he could discover in the appearance of his former subordinate the ravages of Bolshevism.

"Are you quite sure that you aren't just a bit of a Communist?"

"Me," replied Valentin, "I'm a commercist."

"Yes, but to please your customers?"

"I don't have to please them; it's my goods that please them, not me. And after that we went and had dinner in the German pavilion."

"What?"

"We went and had dinner in the German pavilion."

"You went and had dinner with the Krauts?"

"What a blow-out we had," sighed Valentin.

"You aren't fussy. It would take a fortune to get me to set foot there. And what did you eat? Sauerkraut?"

"The sauerkraut to end all sauerkrauts. And even though Paul's rolling in it at the moment, he made a pretty sour face when he saw the prices on the menu. Have you ever had caviar?"

"Never even heard of it."

"We wanted to try it, Julie and I. Julie, that's my wife. Her first names are Julia Julie. Sometimes I call her one, sometimes the other. Makes a change. As I was saying, then, Julie and I wanted to try some caviar. It was all the more interesting in that it cost, per portion, what it takes me a day to earn in my business."

"You're joking."

"After I've paid my taxes? The net profit? Not really. But Paul told us that only Russians could eat muck like that. Finally we dropped the idea, even Julia, and yet Julia usually, Paul only has to say something for her to maintain the opposite. He fooled her over the caviar in the end, I admired him for that. But it took long enough! All this time the waiter that they called a maître d'hôtel in German was standing there with his notebook and a little pencil. No idea what he made of our funny jokes, in any case he didn't open his mouth, he was as stiff as a streetcar track and as serious as a clockhand, the minute one. The hour-hand is more amusing, it's sort of plump, it takes things easy, it always catches up with the other one in its own good time. When I'm sitting at my cash desk I can see the hands of the clockmaker's clock over his shop. When I haven't got a lot to do, I watch them."

He stopped talking.

"You've gotten very chatty," said Top Sergeant Bourrelier.

"Where was I?"

"Still on the caviar."

"Yes, the fellow didn't flinch, obviously a spy, Julia wanted to ask him, but there again Paul managed to stop her. I forgot to tell you that that restaurant is as snobby as they come, the dames in décolletés down to here, and the guys dressed up the way they do to go out on the town, you know, like in the movies, with their ties done up in a bow so's not to spill the gravy on them. Well, have to admit, we looked pretty broke, especially poor Julia, you have to admit that she's hardly elegance personified, so there was one moment when I thought they weren't even going to let us in, but they finally found us a table where we'd be nice and quiet and they shoved us into a corner so well tucked away that it sometimes took the waiters half an hour to find us."

"And after all that, what great speciality did you have to eat?"

"Sauerkraut."

"What did I tell you!"

"Paul ordered a langouste à l'américaine, Chantal an assiette anglaise, and Julie a boeuf bourguignon, so I was afraid I might offend them if I didn't choose their national dish."

"Well, personally, just to make them sweat, I wouldn't have chosen their pig-swill. Not until they return Alsace-Lorraine."

"Didn't we get it back from them in 1918?"

"That's true, I was forgetting. Yes, but they're trying to get it back from us again."

"And you really think there isn't going to be a war?"

"You still don't understand. The Alsatians, they speak German, right? We'll keep the Lorrainers. And it'll all work out peacefully, Hitler's said so."

"What a lot of things you know," murmured Valentin.

"And after the sauerkraut?" asked Bourrelier, who didn't want to take unfair advantage of his victory on the diplomatic level.

"After? I almost had it coming out of my ears. It was so delicious that I stuffed myself with it up to here."

He placed one hand on the level of his Adam's apple.

"All the more so," he continued, "seeing that there was this much on the plate."

He placed the other hand in a position thirty centimeters above the table.

"After," he added, "it was all I could do to get a piece of cream cake like this down me."

With both hands he rapidly described a sector of a spherical disc ten centimeters high, with a radius of twenty centimeters and an angle at the center of a hundred and twenty degrees.

"Luckily," he concluded, "we had a terrific *vin de pays* to help the stuff down. Johannisberg, they call it."

"Baloney!" said Bourrelier. "Pure propaganda. It can't touch our Beaujolais. The Huns don't know how to drink."

"We were really lit up when we left, even Paul, though goodness knows he'd just paid through the nose."

"How much was it?"

"More than a hundred francs a head."

"That doesn't exist."

"Paul showed me the bill. As he was paying, he didn't want us to think he'd treated us in a dump for derelicts. Well, it came to nearly five hundred francs."

"Now I've heard it all! Even so, it's a lousy rotten idea to chuck your cash away on the Huns."

"After, we went over to the fair. There's a whole lot of side shows and things. And then there's the tower, you jump off the top in a parachute."

"How high is it, your tower?"

"Twenty or thirty meters, shdthink."

"And don't the people hurt themselves?"

"They've got wires holding them."

"And don't the wires break?"

"Not while we were watching."

"Did you try it?"

"Julia wouldn't have let me."

"*I* shall try it."

"You're quite right. I'll give you something to do, and it isn't dangerous. After, I had a ride on the rollercoaster. Nothing better, to get the sauerkraut to go down. Drops like that."

He outlines a gradient of nine and a half in ten.

"And aren't there any accidents?"

"Not while I was there. But that's not all."

"Go on."

"Well, can you imagine, first of all I must tell you that Chantal and I had lost Paul and my ever-loving, Chantal, that's my sister-in-law, you know her, she's the lady who came to interview you about me."

"You've already told me that," said Bourrelier impatiently. "Get on with your story, I've got a feeling that we're getting to the interesting bit. I can guess what came next."

"And what have you guessed?" asks Valentin, raising astonished eyes to the top sergeant.

"I'll tell you after. Come on, give."

"Julie guesses everything, too: how many aperitifs I've drunk, how many customers I've seen, how many papers I've read."

"Do you read a lot?"

"Mostly the weeklies. *Marie-Claire*, that's a must because of the business. And then especially *Hop-là* and *Robinson*. The newspapers I buy are the *Petit Parisien* for Julie and *L'Auto* for me."

"Are you going in for sports, now?"

"Have to, because of the customers."

"Which sports?" asked Bourrelier.

"None! No, I just keep up to date. True though, on Sundays, that would help me pass the time."

Having ventilated this possibility, Valentin allowed himself to graze dreamily the prairies of the imagination.

"Come on, get back to your story," said Bourrelier.

"Well, as I was saying, Julia guesses everything. Even when

110

she makes a mistake, she's still guessed something. Other times she doesn't guess anything."

And once again he allowed himself to go tripping through the lucerne of dreams.

"Hold it," said Bourrelier, "you haven't finished the other one. With your sister-in-law in the rollercoaster."

"That's right. I'll tell you all about it."

"Gwon then."

"Well, seeing that we'd lost the others, we treated ourselves to a ride, me and Chantal. They're pretty narrow, those little cars, you know what I mean, they bring you together."

"I understand."

"We had another ride. That brought us even closer together. After, we were rambling around laughing, not even bothering whether we met up with the others. It's full of dark corners, the Expo, I warn you, and it was odd how we kept finding ourselves in these dark corners. And then I put my hands round her a bit."

He looked at the top sergeant inquisitively and asked him:

"You get me?"

"Go on, go on."

"And then, I kissed her."

"I thought so!" exclaimed Bourrelier triumphantly.

"Is it true that that was what you guessed?"

"Eggzackly."

"Well, really. Because it isn't finished."

"Go on, go on."

Valentin remained silent for a few moments and then, raising his eyes up to the ceiling, he declared:

"She uses a good toothpaste."

With gritty lips, staring eyes and skidding voice, Bourrelier begged him:

"Go on, go on."

"After, as our dogs were hurting, we'd done such a lot of walking, we were looking for something where we could sit down and we discovered the Magic Gondola. They put you in a gondola that goes all by itself, on the water, naturally, and in the dark, what's more. You're in like what you might call a sewer. Every so often you pass a lit-up whatsit that's meant to look like Venice, but apart from that you're all the

111

time in the dark. And you're all by yourselves in the gondola. You get the picture?"

"Do I get the picture!" mumbled Bourrelier, dabbing at his bean.

Being a top sergeant, he had a very well-developed visual memory, and Chantal often replaced one of his partners if she was too hideous.

"Then what? Then what?"

"Well, I took my clod-hoppers off because they were hurting like hell."

"Is that all?"

Valentin was already coming to the end of his story:

"A funny thing happened."

"What happened?"

"There must have been a technical foul-up, the gondola suddenly came into a brightly lit room where there were lots of people looking at us and laughing their heads off."

"And what were you doing, the two of you?"

"We were screwing . . ."

"Well well," said Bourrelier, stirred.

". . . ourselves up into balls, massaging our feet," concluded Valentin. "So we put our shoes back on, and we went out, and the people were clapping. We had a good laugh. A bit farther on we found the others, who were looking for us. And there you are. You'll see, you'll have a good evening at the Expo."

Valentin took out his wallet and called the owner.

"I'm really glad to have seen you again, but I must go home to lunch now. Madame Brû is waiting for me, she'll be hopping mad with me for being so late. But she'll have guessed why. Maybe. Hm, the day of the Magic Gondola, she didn't guess a thing."

"But your sister-in-law and you, do you?"

"Oh well you know, I haven't seen her since. A month later she moved to Châtellerault with Paul. No, leave it. It's all mine, boss. Soldiers aren't allowed to pay. Here, look at this, a brochure I picked up in the German pavilion."

Bourrelier read it out aloud:

" 'Committee for Franco-German rapprochement. Tourist Section. The Napoleonic battlefields in Germany at reduced

prices in a luxury coach. Only the French victories: Ulm.
Eckmühl. Lützen. Auerstaedt. Jena.'"

"I'll treat myself to that one day," said Valentin. "What's
sort of a bore, though, is that I'm only interested in Jena."

XIV

WHEN HE had started selling films, the photographer from the
rue de la Durance had come and explained that he was en-
gaging in unfair competition and Valentin didn't want to
engage in unfair competition with anybody. Next he had
thought of adding a cleaning materials department to his
business, but Balustre who kept the hardware store hadn't
failed to tell him how much that distressed him and Valentin
didn't want to distress anybody. And when he had had the
idea of launching out into fancy goods and Paris novelties,
Meussieu Panneton who was the manager of the Reuilly
Bazaar had dissuaded him by demonstrating to him what
trouble that would cause to the economic life of the district,
and Valentin didn't want to make any trouble anywhere.

So he had to abandon the idea of expanding his trade, and
this was his last attempt to efface his indolence. All he had left
now was the very vacuity of time. Then he tried to see how
time passed, an undertaking just as difficult as that of catching
yourself falling asleep. Sitting at his cash desk he would watch
the big clock above Meussieu Poucier's shop, and follow the
progress of the big hand. He would manage to see it jump
once, twice, three times, and then he suddenly found it was a
quarter of an hour later and the big hand had taken advantage
of this to move without his noticing it. Where had he been all
that time? Sometimes he had been back in Madagascar, some-

times he had relived an episode from Flash Guy or Mandrake, his favorite heroes, sometimes he had merely re-eaten a meal or re-seen a film, more or less fragmentarily.

At the end of two months of application, he managed to register three jumps of the big hand, but he never got up to four, not remembering *this* occupation until much later, being then lost in a fun-jungle, or repeating to himself like a scratched record some conversation he had had with Houssette, Virole, or one of his other neighbors. He couldn't manage to make his mind a blank.

Naturally, it happened that just at the moment when the minute was getting ready to die and become transformed in that little white space that on the circumference of the clock a skilled painter had enclosed within two equal black lines, some person or personess came in with framing preoccupations which obliged Valentin to relinquish his own. The trouble he went to to satisfy them had guaranteed him some very good customers, but he observed that, little by little, they became divided into those who were good, and who bought things, and those who were no less good but who bought nothing. The latter category who, in consequence, weren't customers at all, came to confide in him.

At first they had found him a nice, chatty fellow, with a good head for business. When, on Julia's injunction, he had started to question them, discreetly of course, about their jobs, their children and their indispositions, and then about their love affairs and their financial situation, he had immediately met with a response, and in no time at all he no longer had to go to the trouble of trying to provoke their confessions, for intimate details extravasated of their own accord, and women who came to see Valentin for the first time would immediately acquaint him with the list of their lovers and the state of their finances. In the café, even the most hardened habitués would come and whisper their little problems in the hollow of his ear and, before taking any serious decisions, would give him all the data, though never going quite so far as to ask his advice. He even observed that the more he followed the course of time on the deserted circus of the clock, the more he became the recipient of the outpouring of the banal, incidental, or secret news items that Julia subsequently and voraciously reingurgitated. For he was not only supposed to listen, but also to repeat.

In the evenings, after they'd polished off the leftovers from lunch, Valentin took the leftover leftovers back to the kitchen and Julia started to drink coffee, a substance whose peculiarity was that it made her sleep. And while Valentin was talking, she would noisily consume two or three cups of the said substance which she sugared profusely. He would pour himself out some *eau-de-vie* in a small, thick, heavy, conical glass of which he was very fond and which he only emptied when the session was over, and then at one gulp.

"Things aren't going so well with the Viroles," said Valentin.

"No? What's wrong?"

"There's trouble brewing. Virole told me all about it just now."

"Has he knocked up the maid?"

"Not exactly. I mean: actually, yes, but some time ago. He's got a sixteen-year-old daughter, whose existence his old woman didn't know the first thing about. He had her when he hadn't even been married three years. He's giving her a good education, she's just about to take her *baccalauréat*. He hasn't dropped the mother, either, he makes her a small allowance."

"So that was what was making a hole in their budget, that Madame Virole couldn't make out."

"How d'you know that?"

More and more often, his monologues were turning into dialogues, and Valentin wondered where on earth Julia could have heard this or that bit of gossip when she never went out and never saw anyone. The reply was always the same:

"Don't you remember? You told me yourself."

This time he *did* remember. He had never told her any such thing. What was more, this time he had really been paying attention:

"But why did you say: *so that* was what it was? Why *so that?*"

He even dared look at her insistently and inquisitorially. She was well aware that one day he would understand, or guess, but she found it infinitely amusing to delay that moment. And then, he wouldn't find out *everything* at one crack, what he did discover might well satisfy him for a time, and the rest would still escape him until a certain incident occurred, or perhaps for ever. She suddenly thought that his for ever would no doubt be longer than hers, if the for ever began at this very moment. She saw him, still so young, and she was gripped by fear and envy and pity, and her heart started beating more slowly, to the slow-motion rhythm of unhappiness.

"Well?" said Valentin.

For the first time since she had known him there was an irritated, authoritarian nuance in his voice which was very "husbandlike." And as it was precisely their own relationship that she had been considering so seriously, *this* struck her as comic.

"What on earth are you worrying about?"

As he was terribly ashamed of the "husbandly" way in which he had asked his question, he lowered his eyes and answered:

"Nothing."

Julia came back to Madame Virole.

"How did she find out?"

"Madame Saphir put her on the track."

"Who?"

"Madame Saphir, the clairvoyante in the rue Taine. She set up shop there about six months ago and all the old girls in the district go and consult her. Haven't *you* been?"

"I'm not an old girl," said Julia.

"In any case," Valentin went on, without pressing the point, "old mother Virole is going to send everyone in the district to her. She even tried to force me to go."

"Whatever for?"

"For everything. Health, business, love, luck. But personally I don't believe in such things, and what's more I don't give a damn."

"How right you are."

"Have you really never been, yourself?" he asked once again, timidly.

"Wouldn't I have told you?"

Valentin didn't seem to have heard this answer into which Julia had injected, not without effort, a slightly touchy note. With a faraway look, he declared:

"What amazes me is that people never get tired of going

on about their miserable little personal affairs. When I heard that this clairvoyante had set up in the district I told myself that they wouldn't need me any longer, but it's just the opposite. More and more people come all the time, and I sometimes wonder whether they haven't come to the wrong address."

"Even so, you don't predict their future, do you?" asked Julie, worried.

"Of course I don't tell their fortunes."

He added:

"But I wouldn't find it difficult. Tisn't the same thing. When they come to me, people don't realize that they're disclosing their private lives."

He thought a bit more:

"It's true that when they go and see the old girl in the rue Taine they want *her* to disclose it to them. They don't reveal their secrets to a clairvoyante, they expect to hear them from her."

He concluded:

"It isn't at all the same thing."

"Of course it isn't," Julia hastened to agree; she had been observing Valentin's train of thought with some anxiety.

She didn't guess that he only allowed people to see what suited him, and that he had experimented far enough in this direction to have acquired certain precise knowledge. Even though he couldn't manage to misinform her about how the business was going or about how many rounds he paid for or got given, he had finally become convinced that she couldn't penetrate into the interior of his skull and that, even if the little voice that rises directly up from the bottom of the throat to the brain without passing by the ear said black, the outloud voice could declare white without Julia noticing.

"And what else?" she asked. "You saw six people today, didn't you?"

Quite true; he'd seen six people.

So he picked them out again, one by one, from the basket of his memory, shook them up so as to separate out the small change of their existence, and then threw them back into the well of Mnemosyne.

His task is completed. Julia can go to bed. So can he.

He slowly finishes his second cigarette of the day. He asks:

"Haven't any idea where we'll go for our vacation this year, have you?"

"No. Couldn't care less."

"The first year, I went to Bruges on my own."

"That wasn't a vacation."

"You didn't have one at all. Last year we stayed at home because of the Expo. Wouldn't you like us to go away together?"

"But of course I would, sweetheart. Then you've got an idea, have you?"

She'd guessed correctly that he had an idea, but not what it was, and, as happened every time that he observed this phenomenon, it made Valentin rather proud.

"Why shouldn't we go to Germany?"

"I'm quite willing," Julia replied at once. "I really couldn't care less: here or there."

"I've discovered an interesting package tour," he said, bringing a bit of paper out of his pocket. "A week in a luxury bus, and not expensive. Would you like that?"

"I keep telling you: I couldn't care less. If it's within my price range, we'll treat ourselves to it."

"I'm so glad," said Valentin. "That's decided, then?"

"Yes, sweetheart."

"Though by the way," said Valentin, "I don't really believe we'll go. There'll be a war before then."

"Of course there won't, you poor dope. There won't be a war, I tell you. Why do you always come out with such crazy ideas?"

Valentin had let this reservation escape him, but these days he refrained from any sort of allusion to this subject with all and sundry. Which only made them like him more.

Lying on his back, he was now trying to discover the difference between thinking of nothing with your eyes closed, and being in a dreamless sleep. As usual, the result of this effort is that he wakes up immediately, nine hours later, and then, the whole morning, he finds himself sweeping, polishing, cleaning, and even sometimes selling. It's especially in the afternoons that he is able to devote himself to following the movement of the clock-hand, with his mind clear of the pictures that everyday life deposits in it. Valentin, looking intently at the dusty

118

clock, doesn't feel in the least empty. Clusters of common-place words go crackling through a wasteland of automatic movements or of colorless objects, but this doesn't make a desert. The tone of voice in which Balustre had said to him this morning: "I've got some enamel paint for your silver frames" enables this phrase to reverberate indefinitely with the obsessional rigor of Dutchwomen demanding their cocoa. And Valentin starts observing this echolalia which comes to dismiss, he doesn't know why, a deep, anonymous voice that is im-periously demanding "gum, gum, gum," and which departs between two lines of identical Balustres and then disappears into the distance with the flabby sound of a floorcloth falling into the bottom of an empty bucket. In the meantime the voices become absorbed into their shadows and the various Balustres become obliterated in views of Paris or newspaper photographs, over which are superimposed uninteresting and yet unknown landscapes with leaden lighting: these are forests on silvery nights, or oceans before the storm. Valentin notices that it never rains there. *For the moment* he doesn't notice anything at all. He stares at a branch, or a pebble, but he loses sight of time. Time has pushed the hand on ten minutes far-ther and Valentin hasn't caught it at it. And since the branch and the pebble, *nothing* has happened. And sometimes he finds himself, of his own accord, hanging on to the clock, and at other times even after he has spoken he still believes he is a prey to mirages and repetitions.

As well as the customers who buy and those who don't buy, this latter category increasing every day at the expense of the former, there are the salesmen, the delivery men, the agents of the different government services, and finally the beggars, a denomination in which Valentin includes nuns, collectors, the secretaries of various organizations, dealers in Bibles and pencils, sellers of carpets and Arabian amulets shaped like human hands. He never buys anything, but he's quite pre-pared to give. The Bible merchant is beginning to irritate him, he comes round regularly and has never yet managed to place a single one of his holy books. He's even offered to sell him one on approval; he'll take it back if Valentin hasn't found the solution to all his problems in it. But Valentin doesn't want to know, he offers him a franc; the other is offended and goes away, without taking the money. The Arab has given up oratorical contests; sometimes he doesn't even come in, he's content to smile as he goes by. On the other hand the local beggars come regularly, there are four of them and they take good care not to spread the news among their colleagues in the rue de Picpus or Place d'Aligre. Local patriotism determines the limits of Valentin's generosity, though he doesn't quite realize that he gives twenty sous a day from Monday to Friday and forty sous on Saturday to Père Pommier, to Only-one-bone and to Timothée, whereas Miss Pantruche is content with five francs which she collects at one crack, on Fridays toward three in the afternoon. Miss Pantruche, in exchange, has undertaken Valentin's musical education; having trodden the boards forty years before, she can quaver out a repertory whose last echoes must have disintegrated on the eleventh of November, nineteen-eighteen. This bored Valentin enormously, but he thought that it must be the same in all quarters of Paris; if the papers were to be believed, this was the way lyrical artists always ended up. He had tried to persuade Miss Pantruche of the banality of her case, but he had given up when he discovered that he was distressing her.

Halfway between the full-blown beggar and the seller of superfluities there was Jean-Lackwit, of whom Valentin was extremely fond. Jean-Lackwit, who was an awkward and somewhat xenophobic character, didn't like to see new faces in the district. Valentin had been storekeeping in the rue Brèche-aux-Loups for more than a year before he visited him. But now, a mutual liking enabled them to speak freely to each other.

And so, the less customers he had, the less idle he was. To preserve the necessary quantity of idleness, he decided to reform his matutinal habits. Up at five o'clock, he opened the store at seven, thus gaining two hours in which to watch time, in the limpidity of the morning or the mists of daybreak.

XV

Jean-Lackwit came in, carrying his rush brooms. He put them down carefully on the counter and held out his hand to Valentin.

"Cigarette," he said, without specifying whether this was an order or a request.

Valentin gave it to him, with a box of matches as a bonus.

Jean-Lackwit expelled the first puff through his nose and studied the lighted end attentively.

"Pra, pra, pra, pra, pra, pra," said he. "Pra, pra, pra, pra, pra, pra, pra."

"What did you have for lunch today?" asked Valentin.

"Old ossage," replied Jean-Lackwit. "Old ossage, pra, pra."

"Heh, heh," said Valentin, "you did yourself proud."

Jean-Lackwit slapped himself on the thigh.

"Fantastic," said he, choking with laughter, "fantastic."

He held one finger up in the air, raised a leg and let off a fart. Then, having extinguished his cigarette between two fingers, he undertook its mastication, slowly.

"You'll see," said he, dribbling a bit of tobacco juice onto his pepper and salt beard.

He delved into one of his pockets and brought out a piece of blood sausage, gnawed at both ends.

"Old ossage!" he said. "Old ossage!"

By separating his two hands, he indicated a length of approximately seventy-five centimeters; by describing a semicircle with one of them, that he had swiped it; by a gesture with his thumb, that the victim was quite simply Verterelle, who sold sausages etc. three stores away.

"And you had time to eat it between there and here?" asked Valentin.

The other made a sign that: naturally, of course.

"And no one saw you?"

Jean-Lackwit winked. Picking up one of his brooms he pretended to nibble at its handle, all the while voraciously consuming the small portion of blood sausage that was still extant.

"What a clever fellow you are," said Valentin, delighted.

This is exactly the opinion of Jean-Lackwit, who nods, and sits down, almost replete.

"And Meussieu Brû, how are you, Meussieu Brû, how are you, Meussieu Brû, how are, how are, how are."

"I still can't manage to watch the big hand for more than four minutes," said Valentin, indicating Poucier's clock with a look.

The other, following the movement of Valentin's eyes, remained open-mouthed; but he turned smartly back to Valentin when the latter continued:

"After that time, either it's as if I was falling asleep, I don't know what I'm thinking any more and time passes and escapes my control, or else I'm invaded by images, my attention wanders, and it comes to the same thing; time has run out without my feeling it melt away through my fingers."

Jean-Lackwit nodded understandingly.

"Pra, pra, pra, pra," said he, "pra, pra, pra, pra, pra, pra, pra, pra, pra."

Dreaming, he repeated this phrase once again.

"I watch time," said Valentin, "but sometimes I kill it. That isn't what I want."

The other raised his arms into the air, and lets them fall again with lassitude and compassion.

"It's especially the images that get in the way," Valentin went on. "They come from every direction. There are even some that I don't know. Countries I've never been to, countries that may not even exist."

"All aboard," said Jean-Lackwit, "all aboard, all aboard."

And, standing up, he walked several times round his chair, pretending to be a train. Then, abruptly ceasing this activity, he sat down and once again became a silent listener. Touched by this interlude which bore witness to the profound interest his interlocutor took in his temporal endeavors, Valentin continued:

"There's also sounds, noises, words, everything that enters through the ear. Some of them come from a very long way off, radios that might be bawling on the other side of a mountain. There are phrases that get repeated idiotically."

He stopped, he didn't want to make a faux pas.

Jean-Lackwit nodded and stood up.

"Cigarette," he said.

This meant that he was about to leave.

He expelled a puff of tobacco through his nose and held a broom out to Valentin.

"Buy," he said. "Buy."

Valentin took it and asked:

"Did you make it?"

The other made a sign that meant yes.

"Far," he said. "Far."

"How much?" asked Valentin.

"Twenty francs."

"Oh look here, this is a broom for billionaires."

"Twenty francs."

Valentin wondered whether Julia would guess that he had bought a rush broom from a simpleton for twenty francs. It wasn't sure. Brooms probably didn't come within the domain that she deciphered.

He gave the twenty francs to Jean-Lackwit, who saw no difference between twenty francs, twenty sous, and twenty billions. Valentin didn't want to buy it at the proper price, at least for once. The twenty francs were pocketed with dignity. Jean-Lackwit went off, his brooms over his shoulder, going nowhere in particular.

Valentin contemplated his acquisition with affection. A passing excreting dog gave him an opportunity to try out his utensil on the bit of sidewalk that he considered his and toward the cleanliness of which he often had occasion to collaborate with those officials of the City of Paris entrusted with its maintenance. The result proved satisfactory. From the other side of the street, five houses away on the left, Houssette called to him from his doorway:

"Ought to stuff a cork up the dirty beasts!"

Valentin didn't quite hear this proposition, which he would certainly have challenged had he perceived its significance, and replied by merrily waving his broom like a flag. Which made Houssette laugh, for he was full of indulgence for Valentin, as incidentally were all the other storekeepers in the district.

Having accomplished his task of street maintenance, Valentin went back into his store dragging his broom behind him and giving himself up to some slightly diffuse considerations about the identification of the local dogs according to the color and consistency of their leavings. He went and put his new acquisition away in a closet in the back room, then he came back and sat at his cash desk and, raising his eyes to the Poucier clock, he waited for the skip of the big hand that would enable him to take his departure with it, him toward immobility and it toward its next arrival.

As always, the first minute is the easiest. But after the second, there's the meaning of that phrase of Houssette's. What exactly *had* the grocer called out? Then Valentin distinctly hears a fluting little doll's voice articulating: "Ought to stuff a cork up the dirty beasts." Poor dogs. Next time he meets Houssette he'll say: "It isn't a cork they need, so much as a little basket underneath their tails." That would be more canine, and also it would make Houssette laugh. Valentin is still following the movement of the big hand but he has a strong feeling that he won't get far, he's crushed under the weight of words and images. But when Houssette appears, staggering as he'd seen him do on the previous fourteenth of July, Valentin understands why Jean-Lackwit has given him this present. He knows now that it was a present, and that it was only tact that had made Jean-Lackwit ask for the twenty francs.

Without taking his eyes off the clock, he sees himself going and getting the broom out of the closet. He comes back and, with a single stroke, sweeps Houssette away. He pushes him into the gutter, and the flowing water carries the smiling grocer away. Then Valentin sweeps away the houses, then the sidewalks, and then the gutter itself. He gets up to the fourth minute, very conscious of the fall of the hours. A gendarme goes by on a bicycle. He sweeps him away. Another goes by on foot. He sweeps him away too. Houssette comes back between two gendarmes. Why should poor Houssette be walking between two gendarmes? Behind them, Houssette appears, walking between two gendarmes, and followed by Houssette framed by two gendarmes. Valentin forgets to sweep them away and they immediately multiply like vermin. Following this track, he perceives an army of Jean-Lackwits storming a hill which is being defended by an army of de-capitated men. Valentin makes a great sweep of his broom but he starts too late, bits of images are still sticking to the strands of the rushes, he has another go and this time he's stuck in the mud formed by the images. He can't get out of it. With enormous effort, with method and muscle, he manages to restore the desert, but then he observes that five minutes have passed of which he wouldn't be able to give any account.

You don't always succeed at the first attempt. He knows the theory, now, but he lacks a certain flexibility in its applica-tion, and in particular he needs more rapidity, more intransi-gence. You need to start sweeping right away. A jangling voice starts singing in the back of his neck: "The little lark in," he doesn't miss it, he squashes it with an incisive stroke, it goes pschtt and it's all over. That was the procedure he ought to have adopted just now. He puts his broom away in its clasp and promises himself that he'll do better next time.

A gendarme comes in. Why not two? Upon being questioned by the same, Valentin Brû replies that he is indeed Valentin Brû. Well, Valentin Brû is being brought his new mobilization book. The new mobilization book is pink, a rather gay shade of pink. With blurred eyes, Valentin learns that he is to proceed on the tenth day of mobilization to the tenth colonial depot in Nantes.

"That's really it, this time," Valentin murmurs.

"That's really what?" the other asks.

The consternation of the dealer in frames for miniatures and photographs delights the gendarme.

"War," Valentin replies.

The other laughs.

"Tisn't here yet," says the gendarme.

"Tisn't far off, in any case."

"I didn't come to talk politics with you."

The gendarme is getting irritated with the future private soldier.

"And anyway," he adds, cantankerously, "you've got noth-ing to complain about. You don't have to go until the tenth day, and to Nantes, at that! Did you know that there are some, older than you, that have to go to the Maginot Line, and the first day, at that?"

Valentin was not unaware of this. He tries to find a reason for the injustice that favorizes him.

"Could it be because I was in the campaign against the Merina Hain-Tenys?" he suggests.

"Don't give a shit about that," says the gendarme. "But you've got to give me back the other one."

"It's upstairs. I live over the store."

"Can't you go and get it?"

"Sure. But I haven't got anyone to mind the store."

"I'll wait for you. It can't take you long."

Valentin didn't seem to appreciate this solution. He considered that that made a lousy impression, a gendarme in a store. But what if he turned him into a customer?

"Have you got all the frames you need?" he asked him.

"This is no time for jokes," said the gendarme. "Go and get me the other book, I'll wait here for you."

Valentin had forgotten military life. It seemed a bit thick, a man giving him orders. No doubt about it, war was approaching fast.

"I'm going," he said soberly.

He went upstairs, and into the apartment, the door was open, as he thought it would be, no one was in, except the monster who was somnodribbling in the kitchen, that's to say that, as he had imagined, Julia was out. He had no difficulty in finding his service record book carefully tucked away among a pile of sheets, and went down again. They exchanged books.

"That's a good thing done," said the gendarme wittily.

"Didn't anyone come in while I was away?" asked Valentin.

"No one."

"Things aren't too good at the moment," sighed Valentin. "With all this talk of war."

The gendarme saluted silently and left. He went on to Houssette's, and Valentin waited patiently for seven o'clock to come and then went and cordially suggested to the grocer that they should go and have a drink at the Café des Amis.

"Have you had your new mobilization book too?" asked Valentin.

"Oh, that doesn't mean a thing," replied the grocer.

"In what way?"

"It doesn't mean that there's necessarily going to be a war."

"Of course not."

"If we thought that, we couldn't go on living."

"Naturally," said Valentin. "I can't complain, I'm going to Nantes."

"That doesn't mean a thing," said the grocer. "They can send you somewhere else later."

"Of course."

"And then, if there is a war, we'll be bombed everywhere. You'll see what a bashing Paris'll take."

He laughed optimistically.

"Will you be staying in Paris?" asked Valentin boldly.

"Don't bother your head about me," replied Houssette with a discretion that saddened Valentin.

"Ah well," said Valentin, "at least it makes work for the gendarmes."

"Been a lovely day today, hasn't it?" said Houssette.

Valentin hadn't particularly noticed. In June, he thought that only natural. He answered at random:

"Superb."

The days that pass, which turn into the time that passes, are neither lovely nor hideous, but always the same. Perhaps it rains for a few seconds sometimes, or the four o'clock sun holds time back for a few minutes like rearing horses. Perhaps the past doesn't always preserve the beautiful order that clocks give to the present, and perhaps the future is rushing up in disorder, each moment tripping over itself, to be the first to slice itself up. And perhaps there is a charm or horror, grace or abjection, in the convulsive movements of what is going to be and of what has been. But Valentin had never taken any pleasure in these suppositions. He still didn't know enough about the subject. He wanted to be content with an identity nicely chopped into pieces of varying lengths, but whose character was always similar, without dyeing it in autumnal colors, drenching it in April showers or mottling it with the instability of clouds.

"Something wrong?" asked Houssette.

"With me? Goodness no!"

They went into the Café des Amis and sat down after having greeted one and all. They ordered two Pernods.

"Is it the gendarme who's got you into this state? Personally, that's the third time they've changed my mobilization book; there still hasn't been a war, though."

"An ostrich in time doesn't always save nine," retorted Valentin.

"Relax! Go on, have a drink, that'll make you feel better." They drank, and Valentin made a face.

"You're certainly the first Frenchman I've ever seen make a face drinking Pernod," said Houssette.

"It's because of all those whatsits I caught in the colonies," said Valentin.

"Ought to have had something else, then."

"I wanted to see whether it was still bad for me."

Houssette looked at him gravely.

"You're a funny fellow," he declared.

This wasn't at all what Valentin wanted to appear. He was disappointed.

"No funnier than the next fellow," he retorted somewhat vivaciously.

"Oh! I didn't mean to offend you."

"Me neither, me neither."

They took another mouthful of poison.

"And how's business? All right?" asked Houssette.

"No. Worse and worse. I don't know how we get by."

"Don't shout it too loud," Houssette advised him.

How true. Julia never stopped telling him: whatever you do, don't talk! don't ever talk!

"Well, mustn't really grumble," he concluded, contentedly.

Now, naturally, and from every point of view, he had to ask Houssette the same question. That went without saying.

"And what about you?" he asked.

"Grub," said Houssette scornfully, "grub, that always sells. When business is good, people eat because they're pleased, and when it's bad, they eat to console themselves."

"You think people eat when they're sad?" said Valentin.

"What about the great blow-outs after funerals?"

"That may be because people are overjoyed."

This reply once again caused Valentin to be subjected to an inquisitive look from Houssette.

"Do you think people are all bastards?" said the grocer.

"Oh no!"

"Well then?"

Valentin had no answer.

Houssette went on examining him without trying to conceal his curiosity, and Valentin wondered why he had *seen* him just now between two gendarmes. Was it divinery, like Julia amused herself by going in for, or was it a sort of imagery that had nothing to do with the Houssette who was here and now present?

They remained thus for a few instants without saying anything. They didn't seem to be bothered by this silence.

"And your good lady?" the grocer finally said, "we don't often see her, do we?"

"No," said Valentin, who was amazed to find himself in the situation of questionee, he who had extracted so many confidences from the locals, and even from strangers.

He repeated to himself the Juliac maxim: "don't ever talk," but he felt that a simple no might seem a bit rude.

"She never goes out," he added.

"Has she got agoraphobia?" asked the grocer precisely.

Valentin couldn't remember having read this word in the small Larousse French dictionary. Since Diégo-Suarez, he must have forgotten. If time didn't take up so much of his time, he might start reading it again.

"A bit," replied Valentin.

"You don't have it a *bit*," retorted Houssette. "You either have it or you don't have it. Any doctor will tell you that."

"Yes," said Valentin, "but she's a special case."

He considered that a good invention, but even so he may well have talked too much.

XVI

"AND NATURALLY, it's on us," said Paul.

"It's always on you," said Valentin.

"Always? It'll never come to more than twice a year," remarked Julia. "He's had plenty of time since the Expo to earn enough to offer us some caviar."

A Delage, with a hood as long as that, was waiting for them outside the store. A few local tradesmen had even gone out of their way to study it from close up. Some children, near it, were dreaming.

"I'm not going to get in that thing!" exclaimed Julia.

Valentin, on the other hand, couldn't wait to pile into it.

"People will throw stones at us," Julia went on. "And anyway, do you know how to drive such a contraption?"

Paul doesn't deign to answer and takes his place at the wheel. Valentin sits in the back. Julia resigns herself to getting in.

They drive off in a silence full of grandeur, and Valentin waves to his mute friends and acquaintances. When the car had disappeared, the people went home in silence.

During the journey Julia didn't open her trap, while Paul from time to time tossed a few words into the back such as: "And what about your trip to Germany? Have to tell us all about it! How's the business doing? Where'd you like to go?" but Valentin, completely absorbed in the joys of passive automobilism, only replied with indistinctions.

Chantal was waiting for them at the Paltoquet,* a snob restaurant on the Champs Elysées. She had so much shopping to do, the poor little peke, that she hadn't been able to accompany her spouse to the back of beyond in that remote district that constituted the twelfth arrondissement.

"And how's Marinette?" asks Julia.

"We've sent her to boarding school, in Bouffémont."

This doesn't impress Julia.

"Still as much of a bitch?"

"She's improving," says Paul, all the more calmly in that he feels that Julia has said that without conviction. "What will you have?" he asks one and all.

"A cocktail," says Julia.

The Bubragas don't react; they're flabbergasted.

"What kind would you like?" Valentin asks her, amused, for he only knows this vocable from the recipes in *Marie-Claire*.

"Dry? Manhattan? Pink?" enumerates the waiter.

"Pink," replies Julia without hesitation.

"Four," Paul hastens to add.

"Not at all," Valentin protests. "Personally, I want a fruit juice."

"Grapefruit? Pineapple? Tomato?" asks the waiter who, imagining that he is dealing with a joker, smiles subtly and with complicity.

"Which is the most fashionable?" says Valentin.

"Grapefruit, I think," replies the waiter, delighted to have such a witty customer.

"Give me a grapefruit juice."

He looks at the Butragas, and they look at him. He looks at the brother-in-law's big ears, the sister-in-law's legs, and then turns to Julia.

"So you know what a pink is?"

"Think I'm going to let them impress me?"

In the meantime, the maître d'hôtel comes up with his pasteboards and it starts all over again.

"Caviar for everyone?" Paul suggests.

Julia hesitates. Is it so as to get them to refuse? And if it doesn't bug him if they accept, shall she let herself get stuck with some muck that she may not like? Delicate question. Everything that Paul suggests, she tries thus to outsmart him. As for Valentin, he doesn't seem to hesitate about anything. Anyone might think he's done nothing but think about his menu for the last week. Which is true.

He examines the pinks with some curiosity, and drinks his experimental grapefruit juice. He doesn't think it's very sweet. Chantal looks bored stiff. Julia lacks verve. Each of the other three notices this and privately wonders what the reason can be. Her brother-in-law's sudden fortune must have stopped irritating her. The atmosphere of the family meals has changed, and no one knows why.

"And what about that trip to Germany?" Paul asks Valentin.

Good thing there's that trip to Germany, otherwise what would they talk about? Politics again: home affairs, and Paul now shares Julia's opinions about government employees, taxes, national insurance, and all the rest; foreign affairs, and then, one damned thing leading to another, they always came back to Hitler's innermost thoughts, which each prided himself on knowing, and to rifle butts, the sale of which improved every day, indifferent to the growth of the optimism of some and the pessimism of others.

"A week in a bus," says Valentin soberly.

He directs a tender and grateful look at Julia, who had treated him to the trip. In June he had done his accounts, and found that in the course of the year he had taken in less than three thousand five hundred and thirty-seven francs and 50 centimes. With this absence of money he couldn't reasonably go on vacation with Julia. But she had solved the problem very simply, firstly by raising financial possibilities whose source she refrained from specifying (Nanette's legacy perhaps), next in forgoing the trip: she wouldn't budge this year any more than she had the previous years. After he'd allowed himself to be persuaded, Valentin had been to the German travel agency where he had the great good fortune to get the last ticket, the tour being so popular.

"The other tourists all had white beards," said Valentin, "and some of them their wives."

"Retired officers, of course," said Paul.

"Right," said Valentin, "and all Bonapartists. They put me in the back and we went by Strasbourg. We crossed the Rhine. It's beautiful."

"Did you have a passport?" said Paul.

"Of course," said Valentin.

"How did you go about it?" said Paul.

"Do you take him for a stupid cunt?" said Julia.

Paul didn't answer.

Valentin smiled, and went on:

"First of all we went to Elchingen and Ulm. The 1805 campaign. There was a fellow who was explaining. The little old men were looking at their maps more than anything. As I didn't have one, someone lent me one, but after, when we were leaving . . ."

"Did you go to Berchtesgaden?" said Paul.

"No. What for?"

"Don't interrupt him," said Chantal. "Did you like Germany?"

"There are some old towns. Jena, Weimar. But before that we went to Eckmühl. 1809 campaign. All that, that was victories against the Austrians, I take the liberty of reminding you."

"Austrians, Germans, they're all the same, now," said Paul.

"The tour doesn't go to Austerlitz, because that's in Czechoslovakia," said Valentin.

"What did they think of the Sudeten Germans?" said Paul.

"We didn't talk to the Krauts. They were hellish patriotic, all the little old men, and personally, you know, I don't know German."

"Funny idea the Germans had, organizing a trip like that," said Paul.

"To bring the peoples together, so they say. But it didn't bring anything together. You'll see."

"He can't tell his story in peace," said Chantal.

"Good grub here," remarks Julia incidentally; her benevolence staggers Paul.

"Yes, it isn't too bad," he concedes.

He can't help adding:

"It's one of the best restaurants in Paris."

"Doesn't surprise me," says Julia, whose affability goes beyond all bounds.

It almost takes Paul's appetite away.

"Over there the food isn't much good," says Valentin.

"Well," says Paul, "you can't have both butter and guns. As Goering said. Or was it Goebbels."

"You see," says Julie to Paul, "if you sold too many rifle butts, we'd eat like pigs here."

"There's nothing to say that Valentin ate with armaments dealers over there," retorts Paul.

"I shouldn't think so," says Valentin. "Except at Regensburg, where it was good, and where I happened to be at the same table as some Germans. After Regensburg, we went up to Bayreuth, where they play music, and we followed the valley of the Saale, like Napoleon's army. In Jena they showed us the house of a German philosopher* who, on the day of the battle, called him the Soul of the World."

"Who did he call that?" they asked.

"Napoleon."

"You have to admit that Napoleon, he was really some-one," said Paul.

"To cause such a lot of trouble just to go and die on Saint Helena, really have to be a bit touched," said Julia.

The following day they had shown them the battlefield where, on the 14th of October, 1806, Napoleon had destroyed the Prussian army. They had also taken them to Auerstädt where, on the same day, Davout had gained a similar victory. And that evening they had slept in Weimar. The next day, visit to Goethe's house.

"Ah! yes, Goethe," said Paul.

"Who was he again?" said Julia. "You did tell me, but I always forget."

"The author of Faust, Werther, and Mireille."*

"He had talent," said Paul.

"Seems that he dabbled in poetry, too," said Valentin. "He also collected stones and antiques, he filled his house with them. They explained to us how he adored Napoleon and how, when the Prussians had been beaten, he declared that the only thing to do was to give in and to get in good with the French because they were the cleverest and the strongest. Because the Prussians, talk about a crushing defeat, that's what Jena was for them, something monumental. The Kingdom of Prussia had completely fizzled out and they were thinking more along the lines of getting palsy-walsy with the French."

"That's the German character all over," said Paul.

"Only there were still some Prussians who didn't want to know about the French and who were getting ready to have a crack at them. Goethe, now, he couldn't stand them, that lot. In any case, he was even a personal friend of Napoleon, who'd given him the Legion of Honor."

Paul blushed. He was going to get it, at the next hand-out.

"The fellow in Jena, he couldn't stomach the Prussians either, and they were getting a bit jumpy. In 1813, when they started to perk up a bit, he said, the fellow in Jena, that the German women would rather entertain six Frenchmen than one Russian pig, and three Russians rather than one German volunteer."

"Why did they tell you all that?" said Julie, with hazy common sense.

"For Franco-German rapprochement, I suppose," said Valentin. "But the little old men, they weren't having any. They sniggered, and told each other that the Germans' writers and philosophers, they weren't real men, and that in France no one had ever seen such squirts, not even during the Hundred Years' War."

"There was Cauchon,"* said Chantal.

"In any case," said Valentin, "the Germans got offended, and after that, apart from Lützen, we saw nothing but defeats. They even made us go to Rossbach."

"What happened there?" said Paul.

"The French took a hell of a beating there in 1757."

"1757! Then that oughtn't to have been on the program."

"It was a dirty trick," said Valentin. "And we ended up in Leipzig, where they showed us the monument to the Battle of the Nations. Between the 16th and 19th of October, 1813. Since then the French have never been back on the right bank of the Rhine. The little old men were crying with rage about that."

"If it was on the program," said Julie, with more and more astounding common sense, "they had nothing to complain about."

"They were still hoping that the Saxons would change sides and that Napoleon would finally gain the victory."

"What kids," said Julia.

"Well," said Paul, "all that is extremely instructive."

"Not so specially," said Valentin.

"Why did you go on the trip, then?" said Chantal.

"Have I bored you?" said Valentin, "with my trip?"

"You've told us more about it than you have about Madagascar," said Chantal.

"In Madagascar," said Valentin abruptly, "they replant the dead."

"What?" said the other three.

"They bury them," said Valentin, "and then after a certain time they pull them out of there and go and bury them somewhere else."

"What savages," said Julia.

"It's like in history," said Valentin. "Victories and defeats, they never finish up where they happened. People dig them up after a certain time, and make them go and rot somewhere else."

"It's such a shame he didn't go to school for very long," said Julia. "He could have written for the papers."

"You didn't want me to try and take my *baccalauréat*," said Valentin.

"You'd only have wasted your time," said Julia. "You're a frame-seller; just you carry on being a frame-seller, and shoot your mouth off about all this and that from time to time if you feel like it. But not too often," she added.

"Seems to me you've both changed," said Paul.

"That's true," said Chantal.

"You too," said Julia.

All four examined each other in silence while the maître d'hôtel was fiddling about with the duck, pretending to be a surgeon.

"When Paul gets the Legion of Honor," said Julia, "people won't even notice he's got big ears any more."

"You guessed?" asked Paul, blushing.

"You see?" said Chantal to Julia. "In the old days you'd have brought the waiters into it and said: 'Isn't that right, gentlemen?' "

"It's what I'm telling you, we're getting old. Isn't that true?" she asked the wine waiter who was pouring her out a few drops of plonk,* pretending to be a bishop.

"Oh, Madame!" replied this man.

"Is that all you can say?"

"Oh, leave him alone," said Chantal.

"I'm not hurting him," said Julia. "I'm simply remarking that he isn't very chatty."

"Tell me, Valentin," went on Paul who, out of superstition, didn't want them to come back to 'his' Legion of Honor, "tell me, what did you mean just now with your macabre stories?"

"I must tell you," said Valentin. "Sometimes I talk without thinking."

"You wouldn't be a prophet, by any chance?" said Paul.

"I hope you're not putting Valentin on," said Chantal indignantly.

"No, no, I'm serious, and all the more serious in that personally I don't believe in prophets."

"Me neither," said Valentin.

"But just now," Paul insisted, "weren't you trying to insinuate things, about the future?"

"I don't quite understand," said Valentin.

"What are you driving at with your Jena? That there's going to be a war and that we're going to be beaten?"

Hearing these words, the lackeys and flunkeys fluttering around Meussieu_Butagra's guests became immobilized with horror.

"We're talking about a film," said Paul into the void, with a blank smile.

The reassured hirelings re-immersed themselves in their activities.

"Yes," said Paul to Valentin. "What are you driving at? What does that prove? What about eighteen-seventy? What about nineteen fourteen-to-eighteen? What d'you make of them?"

"You're splitting hairs," said Chantal.

"He's getting worked up," said Julia.

"A rifle butt dealer has every right to get worked up when his bread and butter is at stake," said Paul.

He directed his index finger at Valentin:

"Would you be insinuating that my rifle butts are no good?"

"You haven't even made me a present of a single one," said Valentin.

Paul had nothing to reply to that.

"Hm," said Valentin, "that'd be an idea. A medallion sunk in a real rifle butt. A nice frame for photos of soldiers, don't you think?"

"You won't make your fortune with that, either," said Julia.
Valentin laughed good-humoredly, while Paul dreamily finished his duck.

XVII

AFTER MUNICH, the sale of frames became more and more uncertain; it only picked up a bit for Christmas. Sometimes whole days went by without Valentin seeing a single customer come in, and the local people, having no new stories to tell him except to the extent that they were participating in History, now only rarely came to confide to him the more and more petty details of a life pulverized by newspaper headlines. The framer's trip worried his neighbors. They lost themselves in conjectures about the real reason for such an excursion, and the word spy had even been pronounced. The mystery seemed all the greater in that Valentin's replies to different interrogations left the questioners even more perplexed. After all, even though Valentin had discovered prudence, they were not unaware that he considered war inevitable, and the protracted peace had, for some, diminished the interest presented by his remarks, however vague; and some among these some even thought that Valentin provoked this opinion deliberately. Without the faithful friendship of a few honorable tradesmen such as Houssette, Virole, Crampon, and Poucier, he might even have seen coagulate around him a hostility that his lack of commercial success alone would not have been able to dissolve. On the other hand, the clairvoyante in the rue Taine, who had foretold peace to all her clientele, had acquired such prestige that ladies from the elegant sixteenth arrondissement journeyed to the Reuilly district just to consult her.

After New Year's Day, the sale of frames once more totally ceased. The first visitor only appeared on the fifth of January. Jean-Lackwit sat down and said:

"Cigarette."

And Valentin gave him one. What amazed him now about the existence of Jean-Lackwit was that he had been called up at the time of Munich. Jean-Lackwit went off, just like anyone else, and he even came back. His stay with the Armies seemed to have been idyllic, and you might have concluded from his remarks that he hadn't been sober for a whole week. Valentin now suspected him of putting on an act, or rather he could imagine himself in the place of a local tradesman interviewing him, Valentin, about the trip to Germany, at the same time as he was questioning Jean-Lackwit on his activities as a reservist.

"Happy New Year," he said to him.

Jean-Lackwit slapped himself on the thigh, like someone who's just been told a particularly choice funny joke.

"Have to admit," said Valentin. "This year we're for it."

Jean-Lackwit, who had had enough of smoking, transferred his immediate desire to the act of eating and, as he had nothing but tobacco at hand, he began to consume it.

Valentin watched him doing so and noticed that now he only chewed very small butt-ends.

"They're better when you smoke them, aren't they?" he said.

Jean-Lackwit hadn't realized.

"Happy New Year," he said. "Happy New Year. Happy New Year. Happy New Year. Pra pra pra pra pra pra pra pra. Happy New Year."

Valentin followed his example and slapped himself on the thigh with a hilarious look.

"Happy New Year," Jean-Lackwit went on and, with his index finger bent, he added: "tack tack tack tack tack tack tack tack tack. Boom! Boom!" he yelled with such force that he frightened himself, and went and hid behind a chair.

"It's going to be a picnic," sighed Valentin.

Hidden, Jean-Lackwit was silently trembling, like a dog.

"And then what?" said Valentin.

The other slowly got to his feet and came toward him, wrists together, with the gait of a Volga boatman. He stopped in front of the cash desk behind which Valentin was sitting and, putting his hands on its old-fashioned copper covering which in Chignole's day had known the louis-d'or, he murmured:

"Hungry! Hungry!"

Valentin shook his head.

"And are you going to tell all that to the other storekeepers in the district?"

Jean-Lackwit smiled slyly, and began to recite in a shrill voice and at top speed:

> *A Grasshopper the summer long*
> *Sang her song*
> *Took her tale of want*
> *To her neighbor Mistress Ant*
> *Now's your chance,*
> *Mistress Grasshopper, to dance.*

"Haven't you skipped a bit?" said Valentin.

"Boom! boom!" said Jean-Lackwit again, energetically, and, quivering, he ran and cowered behind a chair.

"I had nightmares again last night," said Valentin. "There was a sort of heathland, I was going toward a village tucked away in this back of beyond, and the village stank. You could smell it a very long way off. When I got there, I found nothing but abandoned shacks, and the streets were paved with decaying animal carcasses. I've quite often dreamed of things like that."

Still hunched up, Jean-Lackwit was silently weeping.

"Do sit down," said Valentin.

The other made a gesture which meant that he preferred to stay as he was.

"Thanks to your broom," Valentin went on, "I've managed to follow time, nothing but time, for more than seven minutes. But I understand now that what I have to do isn't to follow it, but to kill it. After I've got away from myself with so much concentration, when I find myself a bit later on back

140

in the place I started from without ever having budged, is that like when you sleep without dreaming?"

Jean-Lackwit kept mum.

A gendarme came in.

He saluted the proprietor very politely and informed him of his mission: he had come to change the mobilization book of Brû (Valentin). Having stated his desire, which was all the more legitimate in that it did not depend on capricious subjectivity but on the objectivity of the plans for the defense of the State, the gendarme, casting an absent-minded look around him, perceived Jean-Lackwit who, behind his chair, was showing all the signs of the bluest and most abject funk. Somewhat surprised, even though experienced in these matters, the gendarme was possibly about to proceed to a methodical inquiry when he heard himself asked whether he wished to recover the old one. And how, he certainly did wish to recover the old one, that was even an essential part of his mission! He extracted the new book from his game-bag. Valentin learned thus that he was to proceed on the eleventh day of mobilization to the tenth colonial depot in Nantes. He gained a day, but why?

Without deliberately wishing to offend the gendarme, he said to him:

"That doesn't change much for me."

"What do you suppose I care?" replied the gendarme blithely.

The individual hiding behind the chair, however, was spoiling the pure joy that the soldier was experiencing in the fulfillment of his function. Valentin noticed this.

"Atten-shun!" he shouted.

Jean-Lackwit sprang to his feet and proudly obeyed, which induced the gendarme to do likewise.

"Right-about turn, right! Forward, march! One, two! One, two! Open, door! One, two! One, two!"

And Jean-Lackwit, preceded by the gendarme, marched out of the store.

Valentin watched them go. He'll be back, he mused, thinking of the gendarme. He took the handle off the street door and went up to get his service record book.

The apartment was empty, as usual, or, rather, as it had

been on the rare occasions when he had gone to see. He didn't bother to go into the kitchen to glance at the somnolence of the cooking monster and was about to cross the bedroom to search in the wardrobe under the pile of sheets when he found himself sailing across the floor. He had bumped into something soft.

It was Julia.

She was lying there at full length, looking very dead.

That's all we needed, thought Valentin, and he stayed where he was. Then he thought: my life's going to be changed, and almost at the same time: so's hers. From which he very rapidly concluded: I'm not such an egoist as all that, seeing that I'm thinking about her. Then, even more rapidly, he wondered why the word egoist had exploded like that in his reflections. Then he jumped over Julia's body and ran downstairs. There he collides with the gendarme, who looks furious.

"My wife's dead," he told him, "I'm going to run and get a doctor."

He abandons the soldier, who wonders whether anyone has the right to pop off while people are changing a mobilization book.

Valentin runs. In actual fact, he doesn't run to a doctor's, because he doesn't know any. Julia never had anything wrong with her, and he himself suffered from perfect health. Valentin runs to Poucier's to ask for help. Poucier and his wife come charging behind Valentin, followed before long by Houssette and the florist. The gendarme goes upstairs too, to establish his priority. There are now two sufferers to succor, for the monster, coming out of her kitchen, has an epileptic fit, thus revealing a malady that she had managed to hide.

Valentin sees people revolving around him, a pandemonium of active and effective personages. A doctor arrives, he knows not how. Caught up in this utilitarian frenzy, Valentin effects the exchange of his mobilization book and the gendarme goes off satisfied and Valentin congratulates himself on not having been all that unequal to his task.

The doctor then seeks him out and cautiously announces that the lady is by no means dead.

"A little stroke," says he. "Probably remain paralyzed. As for your sloven, she's an epileptic. You'll have to get someone else to look after your mother, my boy. That'll be twenty francs, but don't worry, I'll be back."

"Damn stupid business," said Julia, when she was once again able to express herself a few days later. "You're up shit creek, aren't you, my poor angel?"

"You'll be all right," said Valentin.

"Hell, what more do you want," said Julia, "I've taken a terrible beating."

"I tell you, you'll be all right."

"And the other cuntess who has the nerve to treat herself to the haut mal. You'll have to chuck her out and find some-one to look after me."

"Can't we keep them both?" suggested Valentin, whose heart bleeds at the thought of throwing the poor monster out, and who knows he is incapable of carrying out her liquidation.

"And what'll you pay them with?"

Valentin lowers his eyes.

Julia looks at him.

"Poor sweetheart," she sighs. "Here, this is what you do: you write some notices, big as this, asking for a maid, and you get the local storekeepers to stick them up."

"That's an idea," says Valentin.

And he immediately sets to work.

"Do we put how much we give her?"

"Are you mad?"

"It's going to be difficult to pay her," says Valentin, whose business is still in the red.

"I've got a bit of money tucked away," says Julia. "But it won't last long."

Valentin scratches his head.

"Maybe we could sell something other than frames," he says. "If I went about it a bit better, I might possibly manage."

"You haven't got the head for it," says Julia, stroking his hair.

She sees him in army uniform. But he isn't going past her door any more, he's sitting in a truck, his legs dangling, by the side of other soldiers. Is that yesterday, or for later on?

143

"I could join up again," suggested Valentin, "there'd be the bonus. Whether I re-become a re-soldier right away or in three months' time . . ."

"You're stupid," says Julia.

Valentin doesn't insist. He has some other suggestions to make:

"Paul might find me a job as one of his workmen. Even though I don't particularly want to contribute to the world's armaments," he hastens to add.

"You see."

"Mightn't he have an easy job? A soft spot?"

"Don't count on it. He acts as if he's great pals with you, but he's a bastard."

"You think so?"

"He hasn't been able to stomach you ever since you pawed Chantal at the Expo."

"Did he see me?"

"Chantal told him, of course."

"And you, how do you know?"

"She told me, of course."

How they talked about him! Valentin was greatly concerned. He had a hope:

"Did you see us?"

"We only saw you when we met up again."

Valentin scratched his head.

"Did you guess?"

"Maybe not."

Julia smiled:

"And you—what did you guess?"

"What about?" he asked, surprised.

She didn't answer.

"I'll go and deliver my bits of paper," said Valentin.

He took some time about it, because of the information he had to supply about his wife's illness. When he got home, somewhat fatigued by the necessity of saying the same thing over and over again, Julia immediately said:

"Here, you can do me a favor."

"Of course."

"You get a bit of paper this size and you write on it: 'Back tomorrow' very legibly, and you go and stick it with

144

four thumbtacks on the left-hand door on the third floor, back staircase, of number twelve rue Taine."

"Right away, Ma'am," said Valentin.

He calligraphed the message and, still admiring his handiwork, said:

"Right. Here I go. Twelve rue Taine, back staircase, third floor, left?"

"Yes. But. Wait a moment. You go out through the courtyard. At the back, there's a door that gives onto a cul-de-sac that ends between the timber yard and the boiler-maker's. Before the boiler-maker's, on the right, there's an alleyway. You'll see a blue door. You push it open and you find yourself in the courtyard of number twelve rue Taine. The key's in the drawer, over there, a new key. Don't lose it."

"Don't worry. But if someone finds me pinning up this notice and asks me what the fuck I'm doing there, what do I say?"

"You won't meet anyone."

"But it's lived in, that house."

"When you know how to go about it, you don't meet anyone."

"I certainly don't know how to."

"Risk it; you'll find out."

"What would I say?"

"You say: shit. This is a free Republic, so far as I am aware."

"Not for much longer," said Valentin.

"Have you guessed that?"

"I haven't guessed a thing. It's in all the papers, every day."

"Can you read what's written on people's faces?"

Valentin didn't answer.

"It isn't difficult," said Julia.

"I can read what isn't written on the clock-face of time."

"That won't do you any good," said Julia.

"One day," said Valentin, "I saw Virole between two gendarmes. No, it was Houssette. Yes, Houssette, not Virole. In any case, it's never happened."

"Old ma Virole's got death on her tail," said Julia.

"Did you tell her so?"

"She's been warned."

"I'd never interfere with other people's lives," said Valentin.

"Do what you like."

"What do you mean?"

"Madame Saphir earns pots of money. You're going to take her place until she's better."

"But I don't believe in clairvoyantes!" exclaimed Valentin. "And what's more, I can assure you that I haven't got the gift."

"You'll say whatever comes into your head."

"But it's Madame Saphir that people come to see. They won't come to see *me*."

"They'll see Madame Saphir."

"You don't want me to disguise myself as a woman, do you?"

"You won't be disguised. You'll be very good-looking."

"But my voice, my size . . ."

"You'll wear a veil. I've got a very beautiful one with the signs of the Zodiac. You huddle down in your chair and you change your voice so that it's like nothing on earth."

"For new customers, I don't know, it might well work. But the old ones, they're sure to suspect something."

"Don't worry," said Julia. "When people have made up their minds to be taken in there's no way of stopping them. It's not stupidity any more, it's a mania."

XVIII

On the door, a notice: *Mme. Saphir. Past. Present. Future. If the door isn't locked, come in. Take your Magic Number from the table and wait till you hear the bell ring the number of times that correspond to the said Number. Humanitarian rates.* Valentin pinned his bit of paper above it, at the same time admiring the clarity of the instructions, and marveling that Julia had been capable of formulating them. What was more, he marveled at the fact that he still marveled.

He went down the stairs without meeting anyone, as Julia had suggested, crossed the courtyard of number twelve, rue Taine, went down the alleyway again, then down the long communication trench running along the timber yard, then locked a gate.

Having thus relished the mysteries of Paris, he found himself home once again. Before going up to give an account of the success of his mission, he decided to treat himself to a drink. This time he quite simply went out by the corridor into the street.

He saw a crowd round a black maria parked outside Virole's, which drove off as soon as he had joined the ranks of the curious.

"As if in the times we live in there wasn't anything else to do," said someone.

Valentin saw Houssette.

"What's going on?"

"Virole's killed his wife," said Houssette.

"Well, well," said Valentin.

They automatically made for the Café des Amis. Valentin wondered how he could have known that "Houssette between two gendarmes" meant "Virole in a black maria." He also wondered whether, if Julia hadn't become paralyzed, Madame Saphir would have saved Madame Virole from her fate, or would have warned her of it. And he finally wondered— he hadn't thought of this before—whether Madame Saphir had foreseen the illness that was interrupting her career.

"Well then," said Houssette, sitting down, "so the King of England is going to come and visit us."

"It's a sign of war," murmured Valentin.

But they were carried away by the torrent of the general conversation. What exactly had happened? Which of them was in the wrong? She nagged him, right, but that was no reason to do her in. Such a decent woman! Such a decent man! What sort of times were we living in when such a decent man kills such a decent woman?

"And the clairvoyante in the rue Taine had warned her, she told Madame Balustre, and she told me. She said to Madame

Balustre, she said: 'Madame Balustre, I'm that scared of my husband. Madame Saphir told me. "Madame Virole," she said, "watch out, you're quite liable not to die in your bed on account of your husband." ' That's what Madame Saphir told Madame Virole, according to what Madame Balustre said."

Valentin turned round to see who was so well informed. It was Verterelle, whom a sincere widowerhood had long kept away from the bistros. Julia might have told Madame Verterelle, too, that she *would* die in her bed. But he, Valentin, what would he have been able to tell Madame Virole and Madame Verterelle? That they would win in the lottery and that they'd live to be a hundred and twenty in a villa on the Côte d'Azur? That would have pleased them, but it wouldn't have prevented them from kicking the bucket.

All around him, the conversation was developing into the merry hubbub that great catastrophes give rise to. Valentin saw himself again, opening the door that he thought didn't lead anywhere, walking along that cul-de-sac just behind his house but which he didn't know existed, coming and going in the apartment building in the rue Taine as if he had been invisible. A flick of the fingers had sufficed to push him into a world of shifty and pseudonymous acts. He felt curiously at his ease there and, since Julia was offering him a new profession, he considered that it would be in extremely bad taste to refuse it.

"It's got you thinking, that business, hasn't it?" said Houssette.

"It isn't only that," said Valentin. "Sgoing to be another change in the district. I'm going to shut up shop."

"Not possible!"

"I'm just not getting any business. I've found a job. In the center of town. Until times are better."

He saw that Houssette believed him. Valentin felt awkward, and wanted to undeceive him. He admired the facility with which he had created a little zone of error in the reasonable mind of the grocer. Up till now he had always thought that language ought to formulate the truth, and silence hide it. The words he would use to Madame Saphir's customers, male and female, it wouldn't even be zones of error that they would form, but zones of confusion in which illusion might remain in suspense until the end of a life.

He would tell the first person who came to see him that she would marry an Indian prince. Not necessarily as her first husband, nor even her second. That would open all sorts of possibilities: she could await with joy the heavy consequences of senility. The first customer was a young woman.

"You're going to get married soon," said Valentin in a little falsetto voice that nearly made him laugh.

"I've been married a week," said the consultant.

"That's just what I said. Time doesn't count for us. Yesterday, tomorrow, what are they in the face of Eternity?"

That's one in the eye for her, said Valentin to himself, pretty satisfied with his eloquence. But the girl was tough:

"Madame, Eternity is all very fine, but for me what counts isn't yesterday, it's tomorrow."

"Yesterday counts too," said Valentin. "Without yesterday, tomorrow wouldn't exist."

"In any case, I've been married a week."

"What do you wish to know?"

"Everything."

"That's a lot," said Valentin in a lugubrious voice.

"Madame, I'll pay whatever is necessary."

Shit, said Valentin to himself, it isn't as easy as all that. Julia exaggerates; she ought to have given me a rehearsal before she chucked me into this. Poor Julia, another of her marvelous ideas.

"I'm going to concentrate," he said, forcefully.

The young person considered that quite natural.

Shall I swing the Indian prince one on her? Valentin wondered. That's all I've managed to come up with on my own, could be that it's not enough. Then he realized that he would no longer be able to beat his records on Poucier's clock. It seemed to him, though, that he was beginning to attain a certain mastery over time, but he wondered why a precise number of seconds more, or less, had an influence on what, precisely, was beyond all measure. And if ten minutes were sometimes reduced to the twinkling of an eye, this twinkling of an eye always had some reference to a man's life, with its

149

beginning and its end. The trampoline of time—wasn't it a swing? And Valentin was swinging.

When he found himself behind his astrological veil once again, he saw that the consultant was asleep. He knocked gently on the table several times and announced in a loud voice:

"That'll be ten francs, Madame."

The madame started, plunked down her ten francs, and went out, haggard and staring. Valentin congratulated himself. Not such a bad début, he said to himself, and, following Julia's instructions which, after all, were so clearly explained on the door, he gently rang the bell twice, for number two to come in. But no one appeared. Valentin scratched his head; there were three possibilities: that number two had fallen asleep; that number two had left and that there was a number three; finally, that there wasn't a number two at all, which meant that there wasn't a number three either, nor anyone. In the first case, there was no reason why two new rings of the bell should awaken the subject any more than the previous ones had; in the second case, ringing the bell three times was the correct solution; in the third case, it wasn't of the slightest importance. So Valentin rang the bell three times. A meussieu came in and deposited his number on the table, number two; he sat down with a crafty smile.

Here's one who thinks he knows it all, said Valentin to himself, but how to counter him? What a profession!

"Then you didn't know that I hadn't gone?" said the know all. "And I would prefer to tell you right away that there isn't any third customer. I have a feeling that you didn't know that, either."

"For us," said Valentin, "two and three are one and the same. Time is double: the past and the future, and yet it is triple, as there is the present."

"If you charge three francs for a consultation," said the know all, "and I only give you two, you won't think that's the same thing."

"I charge twenty francs for a consultation," said Valentin, decided to soak this aggressive jerk. "Payable in advance."

The jerk plunked down his twenty francs and Valentin with natural delicacy covered them with the individual's Magic

Number. But in doing so he had shown his hand, and he noticed that the fellow had taken a good squint at it, much interested. Valentin immediately smelt out the cop, and he concluded therefrom that he hadn't really taken very long to get himself pinched. Would he go to jug? Did people go to prison for divinery?

The other was waiting patiently, looking sure of himself and gently ironical.

What a stinking bastard, said Valentin to himself. Julia would have got the better of him. I'm ruining the trade. And he sighed.

"Well?" asked number two.

"One of your colleagues has got it in for you," Valentin began.

"And what's he look like?" asked the other, who could no longer disguise his craftiness.

"Dark hair, a mustache, with a derby hat, an umbrella, and great big boots."

"And a scar on his right cheek?"

Valentin didn't fall into the trap.

"On his left cheek," he said.

"That's him," murmured the consultant, flabbergasted.

"He's going to double-cross you in a case you're both involved with."

"The affair of the saucer thieves?"

"Eggzactly. He'll cut the grass from under your feet, if you don't look out."

"What shall I do?"

"That'll be another ten francs," said Valentin.

The other hastened to produce them.

"Tomorrow morning, at seven o'clock, be outside the Sacré-Coeur, and you'll see for yourself what you'll have to do."

"Outside the Sacré-Coeur?"

"Outside the Sacré-Coeur."

The other assumed a perplexed air.

"You're putting me on," he finally said.

"In any case," said Valentin, "I can't see what you're going to lose if you go and stand outside the Sacré-Coeur."

"Well yes, that's true."

"I'll tell you something else."

"Yes?"

"About your wife. There's a fellow's got his eye on her, one of your colleagues."

"What's he look like?"

"He's dark; got a mustache. With a derby hat, an umbrella, and great big boots."

"Are you sure?"

"I can see him."

"Well then, it's Anatole. I had my doubts."

"Watch him, he's a bad egg. I'm sorry I can't give you any more time. Come and see me again if you have any more difficulties. I'll charge you ten francs for a consultation from now on."

"Thank you."

The plainclothes cop hesitated.

"You ought to wear gloves," he finally said.

"*I* thank *you*," said Valentin.

The plainclothes cop left.

Valentin watched him, through the window, cross the courtyard. He had a feeling that the fellow would go even farther, as far as the Sacré-Coeur.

Then Valentin rang his bell three times, then four, but to no avail. He went and glanced into the waiting room: it was empty. What was it that Julia had been saying, that it was a gold mine? That the waiting room was never empty? He had to wait an hour for number three, who was Miss Pantruche. This was more like it.

"What do you wish to know?" asked Valentin, shouting himself hoarse.

Yes, what on earth could she want to know, the poor old bag? If she wanted someone to tell her about her past, Valentin possessed all the necessary documentation.

"If you are a clairvoyante," said Miss Pantruche, leaning over toward him so as to try and see him through his veil, "if you are a clairvoyante, you ought to know what I wish to know."

And to think that this wreck dares to play the skeptic, sighed Valentin. He had to get the upper hand:

"You wish to know the future," he said distinctly.

152

"That's it!" Miss Pantruche agreed triumphantly.

Now that he had gained her confidence she wasted no more time in concealing the object of her visit.

"There's only one thing I want to know," she said. "Whether there's going to be a war."

So this poor, poverty-stricken old fool was going to chuck away ten francs just to hear officially what anyone with any common sense could tell her for nothing. Aren't people funny, thought Valentin, and then he discovered that the one about "sgoing to be a war" was much the same as the one about the Indian prince. It would always happen in the end, that's unless you turned in your chips first. Valentin tried a new line.

"Don't worry, Madame," he declared, in his most perfect eunuch's voice, "risn't going to be a war."

Miss Pantruche's face fell.

"And me that was hoping," she murmured.

"Why was that?" asked Valentin, interested, and forgetting his role, but the other didn't notice, and answered.

"That would have taught them, all those bastards," said Miss Pantruche. "A nice war to bug the lot of them and kill as many of them as possible. Storekeepers, landlords, cops, government employees, movie stars, curés, cyclists, overboard! overboard! weighed down by a whole stack of bombs! and let 'em all get blown to bits! to little tiny bits! Ah! the bastards! Last year, before Munich, I was in ecstasies. People's faces, it was worth a fortune. Because they're cowards as well, the swine. And then, the biggest swine and the biggest coward, old Daladier, he fixed it. But I told myself that it was only postponed. Then you really believe there isn't going to be a war?"

"It isn't a question of believing, but of knowing," declared Valentin.

"Of course," said Miss Pantruche, shattered.

"Is that all you wished to know?"

"Yes, Madame."

"I'm going to tell you something else: next Friday, you'll have a financial disappointment. You won't receive the sum of money you're counting on."

"Whatever next!"

Valentin wondered what it was that staggered her most: the precision of the pythoness, or the defection of the framer.

"I can't see why Msieu Brû wouldn't give me my five francs," said Miss Pantruche with a touch of aggressivity.

So I'm the only one who regularly gives her her hundred sous on Fridays, said Valentin to himself, and he suddenly thought that it wasn't enough for her to find the store shut; she would be quite capable of going up to the second floor.

"Whatever you do," he added, in a terrifying voice, "don't be too insistent, don't push it. That'd bring you hellish bad luck."

Miss Pantruche, terrified, said nothing for a few instants, then she whimpered:

"I'd have done better to stay at home. You're giving me nothing but bad news."

"I've got some good news in reserve, though."

"What's that?"

"For you, as an exception, the consultation will be free."

"Oh! thank you very much, Madame! thank you very much!"

And Miss Pantruche shoved off without further ado, for fear that Madame Saphir might change her mind and ask for a bit of cash at the last minute. You never knew, with these people.

XIX

HE HAD so quickly become interested in his profession that the next morning at seven o'clock he was outside the Sacré-Coeur. Up at half past five, he had made Julia comfortable so that she could wait for the monster to arrive, and then stopped by at Madame Saphir's and pinned a little notice on the door to inform her clients that she wouldn't be there before two o'clock. He had then bought *Marie-Claire,* after which he took the metro. This reading made him miss two connections, but what did he not learn? A double-page spread interested him extremely, destined as it was to persuade the reader that she didn't know much about Paris, its history, its topography or its sights. Valentin perceived that on this subject, his ignorance was immense. Not only did he hardly know more than a few railroad stations and a few of the streets in one of its forty-eight wards, though on the other hand all the thoroughfares in which the name of Iéna appeared, the plaque at No. 306 rue de Charenton and the Reuilly cemetery, and what else?—vague and rapid glimpses of the Grands Boulevards and the Champs-Elysées, and the memory of some now-demolished pavilions at an Expo, but he was also ignorant of the existence of the Gallic chieftain Camulogenus, the inexistence of the giant Isoré, and the length of the metropolitan railway system, whose services he was at this moment utilizing. He also learned that Montmartre, which was not the highest point in Paris, which rather disappointed him, probably meant mountain of Mars, and that one might assume, without too much extravagance, that a temple consecrated to this god had stood, in the days when everyone spoke Latin, on the site on which, after the 1870 war, the basilica, the consequence of the defeat in 1871, had been built.

Having succeeded, on his third attempt, in getting out at the Abbesses station, Valentin, still amazed by the number of things his (feminine) magazine had revealed to him, arrived, after a few detours, at the Sacré-Coeur. He admired its grandiose architecture, even though he preferred that of the Saint-Esprit, and then, turning round, he saw Paris shimmering merrily in the June sunlight. He had never imagined that it was so big and, despairing of identifying his little house in the rue de la Brèche-aux-Loups, he turned his attention to the domes and steeples, but he could no more give a name to them than to the stars of the night. He had forgotten that he had come here to see whether his client was going to take his advice, thinking that it was important for him to know, in order to become better acquainted with his new profession; he wasn't afraid of being recognized, seeing that he was dressed as after all he always was, with the exception of the previous day, that's to say, as a man.

Having got rid of his police spy, then, he looked long at the city, telling himself with some sadness that soon there would be very little left of it. The two previous wars had left it more or less unscathed. But the next one! He turned round again to examine the Sacré-Coeur, and shrugged his shoulders. He believed neither in priests nor in their claptrap. He merely credited them with a certain taste for architecture, and also, possibly, for music. Turning his back on the basilica, he tried to identify the monuments. The Eiffel Tower stood out, but the Invalides? the Arc de Triomphe? the Panthéon? the Ecole militaire? the Val-de-Grâce? Notre-Dame-des-Victoires? All the buildings for each one of which *Marie-Claire* provided some delectable detail. And, wasn't it funny, the origin or purpose of them all was martial. Even the Sacré-Coeur was linked with the fate of arms. Did Paris always, then, dedicate herself to the god Mars? Thinking about himself, and about his Parisian friends, about Houssette, about Jean-Lackwit, this consideration plunged Valentin into an abyss of stupefaction.

He emerged therefrom a little later with this observation: that he was in the habit of situating himself in the center of the universe, and that he had never realized it. Looking down on all the rooftops of the capital, there was no doubt something ludicrous about going on thinking this. But on further reflection, Valentin saw no valid reason to change his mind. Once again turning his back on the city, he walked back to the basilica and, seeing the faithful going into it even at this matutinal hour, he reckoned that religion must have something to be said for it in so far as passing the time was concerned and that, for people who were somewhat solitary or abandoned, it was company for them. In any case, what he was thus telling himself was only Julia's opinion on the question and, when he had realized this and gone on to wonder whether, by any chance, he didn't have an idea of his own on this same question, he discovered that he actually did have one, to wit, that a religion to, and for, oneself alone, must have its own charm. This prospect made him smile and, as at the same moment he caught sight of his plainclothes cop, his smile took some time to fade.

His client disappeared very rapidly, however, and Valentin had no time to comment on this phenomenon because, going from discovery to discovery, he had just spotted in a square a statue that seemed to him to be sufficiently strange to merit his looking more closely at it, which is what he did. The situation in which the personality commemorated by the statue found himself and the inscription that adorned the pedestal intrigued Valentin intensely, and all the more so in that he was ignorant of everything pertaining to the life and opinions of the Chevalier de la Barre.* He consulted the number of *Marie-Claire* that he still had in his hand but it didn't breathe a word about this monument. It was certainly not for no reason that the statue had been placed there and, as the person in question was a chevalier, and therefore still and once again a military man, Valentin, after some hesitation, supposed that, given the site, it could have something to do with a Mars Enchained, and it immediately occurred to him that no god could be more appropriate to his personal religion.

Whereupon it struck eight, and Valentin lost no time in returning to the rue de la Brèche-aux-Loups just in case, though it was highly improbable, his advertisements had had some effect; with Madame Virole's murder, people had no doubt had other things to think about. When he reached the corner of his street, what he saw standing outside his door was not a waiting line of candidates but the Brabagas' car. This was only to be expected, since he had written to them. But he took his time, going the rounds of the various tradesmen before deciding to go in, on the pretext of discovering the fate of his little ads. In the main, however, he only heard more comments, even though they were fairly similar to the previous ones, on Madame Virole's murder, so he finally made up his mind to go home. He found Chantal and Julia laughing like anything.

"No maids reporting for duty?" he asked, after he had greeted Chantal in family fashion.

"No," replied Julie, laughing.

"She's getting on very well, isn't she?" said Valentin to Chantal.

"She is indeed," said Chantal. "You scared me, with your letter."

"Yes but I still can't move," said Julie brightly.

"How's Paul?" asked Valentin.

"He's working like mad with this rearmament," said Chantal. "He reckons that the French army will soon have two rifles to every soldier."

"They'll have to stick one between their legs, next," said Julia.

"You'll always make me laugh," said Chantal.

"You know why we were splitting our sides when you came in?" said Julia.

"No," said Valentin. "Why?"

"Because we thought it was a bit odd to have an epileptic maid and never realize it."

"It *is* funny, yes," said Valentin.

"And that we should discover it the very day I get paralyzed!"

"That was a great day," said Valentin.

"There certainly are some coincidences," said Chantal.

"He'd like us to keep her on," said Julia.

"You'd be making a mistake," said Chantal to Valentin. "In the first place, it's no job for her. What if she falls on the stove one day, or off a step ladder? And, naturally, you're not insured."

"We aren't mad," said Julia. "You see," she added, for Valentin's benefit.

"I agree."

But Valentin had just found a solution: Madame Saphir would engage the monster to do her cleaning and open the door to the clients. The business of the bell and the Magic Number wasn't all it should be; he was going to improve it.

"How's business?" asked Chantal.

"Worse than bad," said Valentin. "In any case, you must have seen: we're shutting up shop."

"But how are you going to live? It's going to cost you a packet, this illness."

"You'll be able to lend us a bit," said Julia.

"Of course, of course," said Chantal.

"Don't worry," said Valentin. "I've found a job."

The two women looked at him with curiosity, but for different reasons.

"You seem to be just as surprised as I am," said Chantal to Julia.

"What have you found?" said Julia, who couldn't guess what lie Valentin would invent, and whom this amused greatly.

"Don't you know yet?" said Chantal, amazed, to Julia.

"I've found a job with a fortuneteller," said Valentin.

"What *are* you talking about?" said Chantal incredulously. Julia guffawed.

"It's a fortuneteller who has too many clients," said Valentin, "so she's passing some of them on to me."

"Doesn't make sense," said Chantal. "Men never read the cards."

"I'll be dressed up as a woman," said Valentin.

Julia was choking with laughter.

"You don't really expect me to believe you, do you?" said Chantal.

"It's true, though," said Valentin, who was relishing the delights of improving on the truth.

"But you won't know how," said Chantal, seriously.

"Yes I will," said Valentin.

"*You* know how to read the cards?"

Valentin went and fetched a pack and shuffled it.

"Cut," he said.

"You get them to cut twice," said Chantal.

"*I* only get them to cut once."

He put down five cards: the ace of clubs, the king of diamonds, the king of hearts, the two of clubs, and the two of spades.

"A blond man," said Valentin, putting his finger on the ace of clubs.

"But the ace of clubs has never meant a blond man," said Chantal.

"I've got my own method," said Valentin.

"Cuntess," said Julia, "can't you see he's putting you on?"

"What a bastard," said Chantal, furious. "I almost believed him."

"The moment we get a good maid," said Julia, "Valentin will reopen the shop."

"Don't you want to know what comes next?" said Valentin to Chantal.

159

"I don't want to know anything at all," said Chantal.

The bell rang.

"That'll be a maid," said Valentin happily, going to open the door.

"Are you going to let him choose a maid?" said Chantal, astonished. "I don't recognize you."

"Of course you don't," said Julia, "but I've taken a licking."

"That's not what I meant."

"Ah well!" said Julia.

"I'll send you a specialist," said Chantal.

"You know where you can put him," said Julia. "Doctors, they're on a level with, well, let's say crystal-gazers."

"Tell me, there isn't any truth in what Valentin was saying just now?"

Valentin came back.

"It was for the local storekeepers' wreath for Madame Virole. How much would you have given?"

"Nothing at all," said Julia, "seeing that you aren't a store-keeper any more."

"All the same," said Chantal hypocritically, "if he's going to reopen."

"I gave ten francs," said Valentin.

"You're crazy," said Julia.

He'd given twenty francs, but she didn't guess it. Maybe she would never guess anything again, and he'd remain Madame Saphir all his life. It would be a curious existence, but how could he know? He'd have to go and see another clairvoyante; this project amused him.

Julia, seeing him smile, said, using nothing but the resources of pure psychology:

"I'll bet you gave twenty francs."

"Of course," said Valentin, laughing.

Chantal looked at him: he was getting on her nerves.

"You ought to come to us," said Chantal to Julia. "There's a big garden round the house. You'd be properly looked after. We've got servants, there, and not creatures who suffer from the haut mal. You'll see, you won't find a maid, especially one you can turn into a nurse. And in Châtellerault, there's a very good doctor."

"You and your doctors," said Julia, tempted.

The bell rang.

"That'll be a maid," said Valentin happily, going to open the door.

"How much truth was there in what he was saying just now?" said Chantal, the moment he'd gone out.

"How'd I get there? I can't move."

"We'll put you in the Delage. You'll see, you'll be all right."

"You think so?"

"Of course. And it would be only natural. Now that we're the rich ones, I could surely do that for you, Julia, couldn't I?"

"Trying to humiliate me, eh?"

"Aren't you stupid."

"Actually, I've never done anything for you."

"You were nice to me when I was a kid."

"But since then?"

"Oh come on, don't think too hard."

"Do you figure I've got softening of the brain?"

"Aren't you stupid."

"He's taking his time coming back," said Julia.

Just at that moment, Valentin reappeared.

"It was the gas," he said. "I paid it."

"So you can do that now, can you?" said Chantal.

"Not that it amuses me," he replied lightly.

"There's not only amusement in life," said Chantal.

"Of course not," said Valentin, "there's Delages, too, and silk stockings."

"What a cretin he's become," said Chantal, which made Julia crylaugh.

Without taking any notice of the judgment passed on him by a lady the purity of whose breath and the warmth of whose breast he had one—already distant—day had occasion to appreciate, Valentin was considering two problems concerning Madame Saphir: primo, would she one day make her fortune, to the extent of being able to buy herself an automobile carriage? secundo, would she one day wear silk stockings? For the moment she was content with old cotton stockings and bits of string for garters. He had no time to go into these questions more thoroughly, because the bell had rung yet again.

"That'll be a maid," he said happily, going to open the door.

161

"What about Valentin?" said Julia to Chantal. "What shall we do with him?"

"You can well imagine that Paul isn't going to keep him," said Chantal.

"Oh!" said Julia, "here, on his own, he'll be able to look after himself."

"You see, there's something you don't want to tell me."

"It would take too long," said Julia. "Later."

"Well then, if he has enough to get by on, leave him here."

"If he's on his own, he'll get into all sorts of damn stupid things."

"One more, one less . . ."

"He hasn't done so many, so far," protested Julia.

"He's ruined you. All that's left of your business and Nanette's is a closed store."

"Times are hard," said Julia.

"Well, take your choice. If you'd rather rot here, badly looked after by a male crystal-gazer, I'm not stopping you."

The image of a male crystal-gazer made Julia laugh.

"So you believe it after all, eh?" said she.

"You're the one who insinuates things. In the first place, didn't you have a go at it yourself?"

"I've made my choice," said Julia. "I'll come and stay with you until I'm better."

"Ah! now you're being reasonable."

"Pretty unreasonable, you ought to say, leaving Valentin alone like that."

"So what?" said Chantal. "He won't even sleep with the maid. Come on, you've got nothing to be afraid of."

"You believe that?" said Julia. "If you believe it, then I believe it. You know about such things."

"A bit," said Chantal modestly. "A bit."

Valentin came back, looking extremely happy.

"I've engaged a maid," he said.

XX

Using nothing but chance and the confidences he had accumulated in the neighborhood, Valentin got better results than Julia. Madame Saphir's fame never dwindled, and he acquired some new faithful clients, such as Inspector Tortoni, for example, who had discovered the truth about the mystery of the saucer thieves; all he had had to do was to go up the steps to the Sacré-Coeur; the solution had appeared to him in a flash, and he attributed the merit to Brû. It hadn't taken him long to identify Madame Saphir, and he had got him, free, from police headquarters, a permit to go around dressed as a woman, for which Valentin was particularly grateful to him; in exchange, he gave him tips for winning lottery numbers and horses. He also tipped some losers, but Tortoni forgot the failures and only remembered the successes; what was more, all his other clients showed the same good will and this made the profession extremely pleasant.

Apart from the appearances he had to put in in the person of Valentin Brû in the neighborhood bistros so as to keep up to date with local life, Madame Saphir hardly ever went out now other than in her fortuneteller's guise, and he stayed dressed in these clothes at home, in spite of the dangers this involved. It was in this garb that he went to the Sacré-Coeur every Sunday morning to pray in front of the Mars Enchained that dominated Paris. Valentin had rapidly come around to inventing a certain faith in it, so he was strangely disappointed to see the mobilization posters. The customers that the month of August had to a certain extent dispersed came flooding back, and Valentin handed them out the laudanum of peace with the cynicism of someone who once again sees days appear to have no future. As soon as war was declared, Madame Saphir disappeared. Valentin gave the monster a little money, locked the door, and took down the notice.

The next day, Didine found him with his hat on his head and his suitcase packed; he was waiting for her.

"Didine, faithful servant," Valentin announced, "thank you for having kept my secret so well. Here are a few sous to

163

enable you to live until you have found another place. You can go on living here, unless you're afraid of air raids. I'm off to see my wife in Châtellerault, and then I shall join my unit in Nantes."

Didine kissed him on both cheeks and wished him peaceful hostilities. They began almost at once. Since he had arrived‾ in Paris to undertake the direction of the Chignole family business, Valentin hadn't been anywhere by train. He found times very much changed. Naturally there was no question of any sort of reservation, but it even seemed that the travelers' natural place was in the corridors or even on the couplings. People wondered how the seated had managed to get that way, and inexpiable hatreds sprang up between the privileged and the vertical, the latter in general being victorious by dint of continual occupation of the double-you-sees. What astonished Valentin most was that, apart from the children, who had not yet attained the age of reason, the human beings present all claimed to have a right to be respected, and manifested a perverse preoccupation with the defense of their dignity even though, after all, they were still only civilians, and even nonmobilizable. The declaration of war, still without effect, seemed to have decorated them with an invisible Legion of Honor for the wounds that their egotistical susceptibility inflicted on them. They ought to be made to fight among themselves, thought Valentin, while the women were speaking with emotion of the heroes of the Maginot Line, while the men who were going to be out of the way in the Toulouse region were explaining how you defend your motherland even when you are out of your depth, and the ones who were being sent to Limoges were considering the former with contempt, for in that noble city they were going to feel that they were in a front-line atmosphere and would be able to poke fun at the slackers in the funkhole of Toulouse's Capitol.

Periodically disturbed by the Indian file of pisseresses, Valentin tried to kill time to escape from the rigors of a spectacle that didn't amuse him. But just at the moment when he was about to dissociate himself from his surroundings and thus chop a few minutes off the train's scheduled time, a brat, gripped by the colic, would push past him, trailing in his

164

wake an aggressive mother, an irascible father, or a big sister putting on her stuck-up act, but nonetheless disturbed by the events. Sometimes a whole family would march past, groaning, distorted by the majesty of great catastrophes.

All of a sudden, Valentin started wondering about the feelings he was allowing himself to develop in regard to his traveling companions. In the name of what superiority was he allowing himself to make fun of their jitters or to take exception to their moth-eaten pretensions? Sole representative on this earth of the cult of Mars Enchained, sole clairvoyante of the masculine sex, sole husband of Julia Segovia, none of these qualifications seemed to him sufficient reason to think himself on a higher level than these nonentities, these old cows and these snotty-nosed brats.

I'm like them, he told himself, I've been dreading war for the last six years, I'm being mobilized a thousand kilometers from the front, and I'd rather be sitting down than standing up. He tried to get into conversation with a fellow standing next to him, who was on his own, like him, but of lugubrious aspect.

"Superb weather," said Valentin, taking advantage of a lull during which you think that all the bowels and all the bladders of the compartment have been emptied and that you've got a moment or two's peace, but you're always wrong.

The other treated him to a blackening look.

"So I see," he replies.

"When you're going to dress up as a soldier again," Valentin continued, "better to do it on a fine day than in the pouring rain."

"I'm not mobilized," said the other disdainfully.

"Me neither," replies Valentin, so as not to offend him.

Then, discovering another subject of conversation:

"Hm," he remarked, "it's quite some time since anyone disturbed us to go to the double-you-sees."

The man with the blackening look, for whom meteorology and world history seemed far too abstract, jumps at the appeal of the concrete, and straightaway fraternizes:

"Just look at those turds," he says to Valentin, pointing to the eight occupants of a compartment, solidly glued to their seats. "They wouldn't even budge for a cannon ball."

165

"Don't let's exaggerate," said Valentin.

"Risn't the slightest trace of humanity in them," the other continued. "Yonly think of themselves. Ah! poor France! And what about me? Why shouldn't I have a seat, me neither? I'm tired, I am. Risn't a single one of them who'd think of asking me."

"They're egoists, aren't they?" said Valentin.

"Too true: they only think about themselves, not about me."

"And me," said Valentin, "do you think they think about me a bit?"

"What d'you think I care?"

Then, recovering himself:

"Here—might you be trying to pull my leg? You can't catch me like that, Meussieu."

"Do *you* actually manage it—to think about other people?"

"Meussieu!"

"And about oneself," Valentin continues. "That's not easy, either. Personally, you know, Meussieu, I think about time, but since every second is the same as every other second, that means that I'm always thinking about the same thing, in other words, I end up by not thinking about anything at all."

The other looked at him, surprised. Valentin adds, amiably:

"It elevates the soul."

In the meantime, one of the seated passengers had just opened a bottle and was passing red plonk round in a tooth-brush glass. Obeying his orders, a little boy came to offer some to the two gents standing in the corridor.

"After you," said Valentin.

The other knocked back the wine without hesitation, and smacked his lips.

"Terrific!" he called out to the benefactor. "How kind of you! Nothing like a drop of red to make you feel you're among your own kind. Among Frenchmen!"

The diminutive cup-bearer brings Valentin's dose now, and for a moment he thinks of offering it to his fellow citizen; but I shall offend him, he reflects, and he drinks, and he gives the glass back, saying: thank you very much, and now he guesses that he hasn't had the courage of his convictions, and while the guy, in a burst of fraternization, goes and sits down in the kid's place to have a bit of a chin-wag, Valentin loses the thread of a speech aiming at a definition of cowardice.

He found Julia walking with a stick, and greatly delighted by the affluence in which she was living. Chantal was out. Paul, mobilized as an officer in the reserve, would soon be back, as he was needed for the manufacture of rifle butts.

"Did you remember to turn the gas off?" said Julia.

"Didn't need to," said Valentin, "the maid's stayed behind."

"What! have you kept her on?"

"Well, yes. She's a decent girl, she was a waitress in the Café des Amis, the one in le Bouscat, it was my favorite café. She'd been wanting to come and work in Paris for two or three years. She arrived the very day we were looking for a maid, so I figured it wouldn't have been very nice of me not to keep her on."

"You never told me all that."

"Was it important?"

"And maybe you kept the slut on, too?"

"Oh, her: Madame Saphir took her on."

"I don't know, nothing's too good for you when I'm not there. Two maids!"

"Even so, I've got some money put away. You'll see."

He opened his suitcase and brought out a little black bag stuffed with cash in various forms.

"You keep it," said Valentin, "you can send me some money orders."

"You've been doing well."

"Madame Saphir had some good customers," said Valentin.

"I'm jealous," said Julia, making some rapid calculations, "you made more money than I did. In spite of your two maids. What's she like, the other one?"

"So-so. She's called Armandine."

"How old?"

"Twenty-one, twenty-two."

"Did she know what you were doing?"

"Of course."

"And she didn't gossip?"

"Never."

"You haven't made her pregnant by any chance?"

"Come, come."

"You aren't going to tell me you didn't sleep with her?"

"I am."

"You can tell me anything you like."

"Why? Don't you guess things any more?"

"I've taken a licking," said Julia. "The body's all right, it's even getting better and better. But I'd never be able to do Madame Saphir again."

"You'd be able to do her just as well as me, we're on equal terms, now."

"Yes, that's true."

She immediately adds:

"But on equal terms, you do her better. You must carry on."

The prospect of resuming the role of Madame Saphir after the war didn't worry Valentin, because for him there wouldn't be any after-the-war. Or rather, after, there would be nothing. Or again, it was unthinkable. After such a war, there wouldn't be any after.

The extreme originality of the events that followed confirmed Valentin in this opinion. After he had filed the records of three Tahitians, one Indian, and five Dahomans who spoke nothing but the Fon dialect, he was then dedicated to an inactivity that was all the greater in that, once they had been dispatched in varying and, in general, unexpected directions, these isolated soldiers had had no replacements. Under the orders of one captain, two lieutenants, one top sergeant, three sergeants, and six corporals, he waited, with ten other infantrymen, for the motherland to find a better use for his talents and to give some aliment to his function.

After having democratically and jointly devised a system of particularly perfected bureaucratic protection which almost managed to bring about the dematerialization of this unit, officers, noncommissioned officers, and other ranks prepared to spend some happy days. Some sent for their wives and children, others dedicated themselves to playing belote and indulging in alcoholism, yet others gave free rein to their housewifely gifts, and it was in these rooms, agreeably transformed into ovens that, nourished with studied refinement, the members of the tenth depot of isolated colonial troops prepared to spend a winter which turned out to be particularly hard. The excessive cold that even went so far as to freeze various marrows rendered even more charming a well-being that none of the descriptions of the future war had led anyone to expect.

Toward the middle of this winter, Valentin decided to try to become a saint. This seemed to him all the easier in that, only believing at the very most in a false god, and then only so little as to be not at all, he figured that he had an immediate advantage over his Christian co-candidates for beatification, since the hope of any sort of recompense would never come to cast a shadow on any of his acts. Foinard, another unoccupied private soldier, a curé in civilian life, gratuitously provided him with an abundance of popular literature on the subject. In the first days he had managed to inveigle most of his comrades into going to Mass, but that was when they still didn't know what was going to happen. Now that they knew that nothing was happening and that no doubt nothing would happen for a long time, for years, perhaps, the zeal of the catechumens had cooled in proportion to the warmth of the comforts; going to church was now no more than one of the elements of the dominical complex, with the croissants in the morning, the quadruple aperitif at noon, and the vesperal movie. Before starting to step up his propaganda, therefore, Foinard was waiting for better times, in other words, catastrophes a bit more drastic than an insipid mobilization in the Nantes region.

When Valentin had asked him to get him a few lives of the saints, so as to have some idea of the way other people had gone about it, Foinard had provided him with them free of charge, attributing, however, this curious request to a certain perversion in his reading tastes. Valentin had only been to Mass once, and it had bored him so much that he never went again, even at the risk of distressing Foinard. Foinard, incidentally, had not been at all distressed, he had no illusions. He still had none, and could see no reason why grace should have touched this barbarian in the midst of his voluptuous idleness but, as he was anxious to be considered a good pal, he had collected a few booklets intended for the simple-minded and given them to Valentin. The Curé of Ars, Teresa of Lisieux, Bernadette Soubirous, Joan of Arc, King

Louis IX of France, and Denis the Areopagite, as well as Donatus, Rogatus, and a few local ones, were thus suggested to him as models, but he didn't choose any of them. At a pinch he might possibly have suggested to himself the imitation of Saint Teresa, but he decided that he would rather go his own way.

On the pretext of his utter uselessness, so as not to show himself off to advantage, he forced himself to serve the others by taking on the most boring jobs, such as sweeping, spud-peeling, snow-shoveling, dish-washing. The difficult thing was to achieve this without drawing attention to his self-sacrifice. When he managed to carry out the latrine duty daily without Foinard noticing, he congratulated himself on having so unassumingly attained a certain degree of abnegation. Next, he had to abstain from congratulating himself, which became much more difficult. And when he discovered that it gave him great pleasure to clear a path through the snow or to empty the slops, he concluded that he certainly deserved no credit for these activities, and consequently hadn't even taken a single step along the path of sanctification.

And in any case, the life that the little depot led didn't give many opportunities for practicing rare virtues. To refrain from smoking or drinking cheap red wine, to scorn belote or the weekly movie, would only have been ostentatious signs of no real value. Valentin wondered what on earth he could do. He submitted to the captain a request to be sent to the Maginot Line: the captain begged him to refrain, and not to drag the soldiers of this modest unit away from their wives and acquaintances by causing the attention of some fanatical superior to fall upon it. Valentin capitulated to these reasons. Decidedly, all that was left to him was killing time and sweeping away the images he harbored of a world that history was going to rub out.

XXI

PAUL BATRAGRA, dressed in the uniform of an infantry captain, a get-up which moreover he was entitled to wear, Paul entered triumphantly and said:

"I've found him!"

"Go on," said Chantal.

"Have you seen him?" said Julia.

"No, but I know where his unit is."

"Boasting again," said Julia.

"There's no reason for him not to be with it."

"He could have been taken prisoner," said Julia.

"That's precisely," said Paul, "what we're going to find out. In any case, if he's a prisoner, it isn't serious. The Germans are going to liberate them within a week."

"He could have been killed," said Julia.

"You exaggerate," said Chantal.

"He isn't mad," said Paul.

"All the same, it nearly happened to us," said Julia, "when a Kraut machine-gunned us."

"And to me," said Paul, "in the Saar, when a mine exploded in front of my car."

"We shall never forget it," said Chantal.

"And I'm not counting all the bullets that have gone whistling past my ears," said Paul.

"Your ears must have tempted them," said Julia. "A lovely target."

The two sisters guffawed.

"How stupid you are, both of you," said Paul.

"No but look here," said Julia.

"Do you or do you not want to know where Valentin is? Where Valentin may be? Where his unit is?"

"Of course I want to find my beloved again," said Julia.

"Well then, the tenth depot of isolated colonial troops has retreated to a place ten kilometers south of here."

"It legged it even farther than we did," said Julia.

"I see no reason why a noncombatant unit should allow itself to be captured by the Germans," said Paul.

"You say yourself that they're going to free the prisoners," said Chantal.

"They've used up their gas for nothing," said Julia.

"That sort of quibbling isn't going to get France on her feet again," said Paul.

"Hm, she's certainly flat on her back at the moment," said Julie good-humoredly.

"Well," said Paul, "do you want to go and see Valentin?"

"If he's there."

"Yes. Well, do you want to go?"

"But naturally you're going to drive me there."

"We leave at two," said Paul.

"You seem to be very impatient," said Chantal.

"He wants to tell him how he won the Croix de Guerre," said Julia.

Bratuga shrugs his shoulders.

"That's true," said Chantal, "anyone might think that if you were on your own you'd be rushing there at once."

"Maybe," said Paul.

"You're looking very high and mighty," said Julia.

"It's only now that we can understand why Valentin was interested in the Battle of Jena," said Paul gravely. "The France of Clemenceau has suffered the fate of the Prussia of Friedrich II."

"Oh come on," said Julia, "is it the Marshal's speeches that have got you in such a state?"

With staring eyes, Paul went on:

"Will Hitler create Europe, and succeed where Napoleon failed? Or will France, helped by the Russians and the English, rise again like Prussia in 1813?"

"Which affected his brain most," Julie asked Chantal. "The Saar or the exodus?"

"In any case we'll have something like six years to wait," Paul murmured pensively. "It'd be very useful to me if I knew," he added to himself.

"And you think that Valentin is going to tell you?" said Chantal.

"Valentin was a prophet," replied Paul, raising his finger up to the zenith.

"You mean a fortuneteller," said Julia.

And the two women once again laughed like mad.

They were directed to a farm five hundred meters from the village. On the outer fence a wooden signboard was nailed: "10th I.C.D." was inscribed over an anchor. Outside the farm a Kanaka, a private soldier in the French army, was dozing on a bench. He took the visitors to the captain in command of the unit. They introduced themselves.

"Bordeille?" said Paul, puckering up the skin over his forehead. "I have an idea I know that name."

"I have never had the pleasure of meeting you," said Bordeille, squinting enviously at Paul's Croix de Guerre and thinking: another swine of a reservist who had the luck to be in the Saar or at Dunkirk.

"But *I* have had that pleasure," said Chantal.

Well well, said Captain Bordeille to himself, yes indeed anyone might think.

"It was thanks to Captain Bordeille that Valentin was discharged four years ago. Do you remember, Captain? As he didn't appear on the roster, he would have stayed in the army for the rest of his life without your intervention."

"Do I remember!" said Captain Bordeille.

"Well," said Paul dryly, "we've come to see you about the same Private Brû. He does belong to your unit, does he not?"

"Yes, or rather, he did."

"Is he dead?" exclaimed Julia.

"No, I demobilized him."

"And has he left?" asked Paul.

"Yesterday."

"Ah," exclaims Paul, "I was quite right to be in a hurry."

"You weren't in enough of a hurry," said Chantal.

"And where did he go?" asked Julie.

"He gave an address in Toulouse, which was that of one of his comrades, but he was intending to go back to Paris. What a guy," Bordeille added.

"Why 'what a guy'?" asked Paul severely.

"Yes, why?" said Bordeille.

"*I*'m the one that's asking *you*," said Paul.

"Seeing that he's your brother-in-law," said Captain Bordeille shrewdly, "you must know him as well as I do, if not better."

"He didn't tell you what he was going to do in Paris?" said Julia.

"My goodness no."

"Was he in good health?"

"Excellent. He bore with admirable abnegation the rigors of a difficult withdrawal."

"Were you machine-gunned?" asks Julia.

"My goodness. Not exactly."

"Well, *we* caught it all right," said Julia. "And we were only civilians, I beg to remind you. There were corpses at the side of the road. Have you ever seen any corpses, Captain?"

"But naturally, Madame!"

"Yes, maybe," Julia conceded. "But corpses of civilians?"

Bordeille was embarrassed.

"You see, Madame," he tried to explain, "in the colonies, in Morocco, for instance, it's rather difficult to tell the difference, with the natives, between civilians and soldiers."

"You see," said Julia, "the Krauts take us for Wogs."

"And what did he think about the war?" asks Paul.

"Did he tell your fortune?" asks Julia.

"What a stupid question," says Paul.

"You hear how he treats his sister-in-law," says Julie to Bordeille. "He's a captain, and he's as rude as a pig. Not surprising that we got a drubbing."

"You're forgetting," says Paul, "that *I* have set foot on German soil."

"Not for long."

"Well, are you going to let the captain speak?"

"I don't give a shit what he might say," said Julie, standing up. "What I want is for you to take me to Toulouse so that I can find my Valentin."

"Toulouse is a big place," said Chantal.

"Meussieu will give us the pal's address," said Julia.

"I hope he'll be more successful in his search than he was last time," said Chantal.

"Oh Madame," said the captain, "I haven't mislaid a single soldier during the whole of this war, and I assure you that, during the retreat, that was very meritorious."

"Don't worry," said Julia, "they're sure to decorate you in the end. Where is he, then, my Valentin?"

"Valentin Brû declares his intention to withdraw to the domicile of Madame Teulat, 10 rue Raymond–IV," Captain Bordeille read. "Rue Raymond–IV is near the Matabiau station and Madame Teulat is the aunt of the Abbé Foinard, one of my poilus. Brû and he left together. Yesterday."

"I'm surprised that Valentin should have become pals with a curé," said Julia.

"In this war, we'll have seen everything," said Chantal.

"Yes," said Paul, "what did he think about the war?"

"Brû?"

"Yes, Brû. Of course, Brû. What did Valentin Brû think about the war, that's what I'd like to know."

And Paul leant over toward Bordeille, who emitted an affected little laugh.

"Well?"

"Well, he said that the English would win, because they're the strongest."

"Not possible," said Paul, overwhelmed.

"He's a joker all right," said Bordeille, smiling amiably in the direction of the ladies.

"And are you sure you didn't misunderstand him?" said Paul.

"Captain, do you take me for an imbecile?"

"And he didn't say how long it would take the English to win?"

"Your husband seems to believe these wisecraps," said Bordeille, still smiling, to Chantal.

"Answer me," said Paul, "it's important."

"He said that it would still go on for quite some time."

"Ah," said Paul.

"Don't talk so much," said Julia, "you bug us with all your songs and dances, we don't give a sausage for them."

"And the Americans," said Paul, "what did he say about them? What are they going to do?"

"They're going to raise hell," replied Julia. "Come on, come on," she said, clutching at her brother-in-law, who was in despair at not learning more about world history. "I can't wait to see my little husband."

But the little husband had already left.

"Immediately after lunch," said the Abbé Foinard, who had

175

already resumed the cassock. "He's gone to the station. They say there's a train going to Paris."

"I'll take it, too," said Julia.

"You haven't got your suitcase," said Chantal.

"Couldn't care less. Let's go."

"Excuse me, Meussieu l'Abbé," said Paul, "you were a close friend of Valentin Brû, weren't you?"

"Oh, friend, that's saying a lot, rather what you might call a 'regimental pal.'"

"Well," said Julia to Paul, "are you coming?"

"This somewhat, shall we say, arid, answer, may well surprise you coming as it does from an ecclesiastic, what am I saying: from a Christian. But, I would say, you know him as well as, even better than, shall we say, I do, seeing that you're his brother-in-law, as you say, and you will understand, you must admit, what I mean."

"Fat lot of good that's done you," said Julie to Paul. "We're going to miss the train."

"Have no fear, Madame, it doesn't leave before seven, and, more likely, toward midnight."

"There, you see," said Paul.

"Yes, but personally," said Julia, "I want to have a seat. Because you know," she added for the Abbé's benefit, "you see me walking now, but last year I was paralyzed. So I've got to have a seat. Incidentally," she said to Chantal, "I'm going to start walking with sticks again, and there's sure to be some good-natured prick who'll give me his seat."

"Julia!" said Chantal severely. "In front of Msieu l'Abbé!"

"Oh, he's heard worse," said Julia.

"I must admit," Foinard admitted.

Bolucra, taking advantage of a tenth of a second's silence, asks him a question:

"And what did he think about the war?"

"About the war, or about the armistice?"

"Here we go again," said Julia.

"Well, about what's going to happen now?" said Paul.

"Well," said the Abbé, "he was like everyone else: he had no idea."

"You really think so?" said Paul.

"Your brother-in-law," said the Abbé, "was, in his own

176

way, as one might say, a sort, I won't say of saint, since they only exist in our religion which, as you know, is apostolic and Roman, but, shall we say, a sort of ascetic."

"Of *what?*" said Julie, indignant.

"Shut up," said Paul.

"You'll never get me to shut up," said Julie.

"Are you sure that he never spoke to you about coming events?" said Paul, shouting more loudly than Julia.

"If your brother-in-law," said the Abbé, "was attempting to practice some kind of spiritual exercise that we might call, let's say, a sort of ascesis, very dangerous for an atheist because it runs the risk, we might say, of bringing him back to God, which we christians wouldn't complain about."

"Oh, shit," said Julia.

"God bless you," replied the Abbé. "Or to alienate him from him for ever, but it must nevertheless be said that the benign atheist, of the Valentin Brû type, is in fact forever alienated from him if, as I was saying, my comrade was attempting, as I have already said, a sort of ascesis, but at least, and I may state this positively, he never had any pretensions to the gift of prophecy."

"That's where you're dead wrong," said Julia.

"*Errare humanum est,*" said the Abbé, in an esperantist voice.

"Hear that?" said Julie to Paul, "you're irritating this man with your questions, you're making his Latin all Greek to him. Come on, let's get going. Quick, quick. Thanks all the same," she said to Foinard.

"Don't forget your sticks," replied the curé.

But she didn't need to bother. Whereas Valentin would have had difficulty in finding a place in an empty conveyance, Julie occupied a window seat in a chockfull train which was still chocking itself even fuller. Paul and Chantal went running hither and thither to try and find Valentin in the mob, but without success. In spite of everything, Julia still wanted to go back to Paris, even without any luggage, seeing that Valentin was going there too, and if it wasn't today then it would be tomorrow that she would be reunited with him.

On the platform, an immense crowd went on seething, but an empty train came and stopped on the other track, and the attack began. A savage struggle broke out between the acrobats, the strong-arm men and the know alls, while the old men and the pregnant women courageously tried their luck. Julia was rejoicing in this side-splitting spectacle when all of a sudden she caught sight of Valentin. Valentin too was watching this comedy, impassive and immobile. Julia didn't react immediately, then she almost called out to him, but restrained herself. Valentin had, in fact, just got moving, and had started on a skillful maneuver. Three girls, inexplicably dressed as mountaineers, were taking advantage of the respectability of this costume to try and climb into a compartment through the window. Valentin had gone up to them and was courteously helping them in this enterprise.

Julia choked with laughter: it was so as to get his hand on their behinds.

NOTES

3	President Fallières	President of France from 1906 to 1913.
15	*Vin blanc gommé*	White wine with sugar. Popular around the time of the Second World War, but now hardly known.
34	The Merina	One of the peoples of Madagascar.
	Hain-Tenys	Not a people or a tribe, as Queneau incites us to believe, but a Madagascan poem declaimed "in the form of oratorical duels in which the adversaries challenge each other in harmonious verse."
38	Drouant	Luxury restaurant where the members of the Académie Goncourt (Queneau was one) meet every November to award the annual Goncourt prize.
106	A Hova	The Hovas are the second highest caste of the Merinas—the caste of "free men."

	A Sakalava	The Sakalavas are a quite different Madagascan people.
130	The Paltoquet	A *paltoquet* is actually a lout. But are we meant to think of the elegant Champs-Elysées restaurant, Fouquet's?
134	A German philosopher	Hegel? (He was teaching in Jena at the time.)
	Goethe . . . Faust, Werther, and Mireille	All three were made into French operas, of course, but Goethe had nothing to do with Mireille, whose libretto was based on a poem by Mistral.
135	Cauchon	(*c.* 1371–1442) Bishop of Beauvais. "Coveting the Archbishopric of Rouen, he asserted his right to put Joan of Arc on trial, and resorted to the meanest infamies in order to secure her condemnation." (He didn't get his archbishopric, though. In fact, he got excommunicated.)
136	Plonk	Any cheap wine.
157	The Chevalier de la Barre	(1747–66) Accused of mutilation of a crucifix and of blasphemy, he was executed in Abbeville, but "rehabilitated" in 1793.